BOOK TWO OF THE CELTIC PROPHECY

RELIQUARY'S
CHOICE

by
MELISSA MACHIE

Can't Put It Down Books
An Imprint of
Open Door Publications

I0625773

Reliquary's Choice
Book Two of The Celtic Prophecy
Copyright 2016 by Melissa Macfie

ISBN: 978-0-9972024-4-1

Published by
Can't Put It Down Books
An imprint of
Open Door Publications
2113 Stackhouse Dr.
Yardley, PA 19067
www.CantPutItDownBooks.com

Cover Design by Genevieve Lavo Cosdon,
www.lavodesign.com

This book is dedicated to my husband, Donald,
my very own romantic Scottish hero.

Have faith,
even when things look the bleakest,
there is always a choice.

PROLOGUE

THE WICKED EDGE of the curved blade glinted in the meager light shed by the candles. Cormac hardened himself against the revulsion and fear of the Oracle's feather-light touch. The popping of stitches, a sharp *burrup,* rent the air. He'd have torn the shirt off over his head if he did not know that it would destroy her ability to scry for Sinclair and the would-be priestess. He wrestled with his will to keep his composure when she was so near. He fought to maintain his breathing, fought against the shaking and increased heartbeat. He could not reveal his vulnerability. He knelt so she could lift the remnants of the shirt off his shoulders as if it were some holy artifact.

The Oracle's dead eye rounded on him. He didn't know if she could see out of it, but it was unnerving. The white sclera, still oozing mucus, pinned him to the spot. He had no choice but to focus on it.

"Ye fear me, Master Bard. As well ye should."

Cormac gulped, his mouth devoid of saliva.

"I will ha' their location soon. Prepare yer acolytes. We willna be thwarted again."

CHAPTER 1

Brenawyn,

My lovely child.

I'm set upon a course from which there is no return. I have pitted myself against your father. Find it in your heart to forgive me. Someday.

I have dreams. Terrible dreams. Prophetic visions more like. Headaches—migraines with searing pain, followed by nose bleeds, dreams, blacking out, vomiting. I have never had visions before. I don't know of anyone who has. I am afraid to ask, in case it gets back to him, your father.

These dreams, filled with blood and pain, seeing people slaughtered, sacrificed. Blurred images of a hunt. No leads though. They don't seem to know where to start.

Hunting throughout the years, throughout the centuries. Doesn't make sense. But I feel they are hunting for you.

Choices to be made.

I haven't helped. I haven't prepared you. I've hindered and perhaps I've signed your death certificate. Did a botched job of binding your magic. Should have consulted Mom, your grandmother. She wouldn't have done it. Too late.

I have seen a glimmer. Only if you choose the right path the world will be yours. Not in the clichéd way, but you're meant for bigger things. You weren't supposed to be born now. Or to me. You're out of place, lost in the universe.

I'm begging.

Choose to live.

Slamming the book closed, Brenawyn slapped it on the nightstand and vaulted off the bed. She felt like a bee in a jar. Trapped. Waiting. She had thought that reading her mother's diary would take her mind off of things she couldn't understand, but yet reading had brought it all home. Her mother, if she hadn't been crazy, had seen visions. Did Brenawyn believe in that? What did the Church say about that?

Brenawyn shook her head to clear it. "You were off your rocker, lady." She looked around the room for distraction. She spied the boxes she'd hauled from Jersey to her grandmother's store in Salem and now to the farmhouse in the New York countryside where she had taken refuge. She wrestled one of the boxes down from the closet shelf and hefted it to the bed. She never thought she'd admit it, but thinking about her dead husband Liam was preferable to worrying about Druid lore, visions and prophecies, and of course, the Order, an ancient group of Druids who seemed to have gotten her confused as the central character in some ancient prophecy.

When she lifted the lid, mustiness wafted out; the box had been stored for the three years since Liam had died in a car accident in New Jersey. The smell made her crinkle her nose. A fat envelope lay on the top with photographs spilling out. She picked them up, recognizing the first Christmas she and Liam had shared together. The camera caught Liam in the middle of laughing at something; she couldn't recall what. She'd always loved his smile, she thought, running her finger lovingly over the photo. It was what had attracted her to him at the first. He had a stern face, but when he smiled—oh, Lord, he had a smile that would make an old woman blush.

Brenawyn leafed through the photos. There were pictures of their honeymoon to Niagara Falls, pictures of their house, even before and after shots of the renovations to the living room. Familiar faces of friends peered out from the surfaces in chronological order. The organization did not surprise her: Liam had always forced orderliness on life. Yes, they were all in order, except for two pictures that were stuffed into the middle of the stack, pictures Brenawyn had never seen before.

In the first, Liam cradled a pretty blonde in his arms. The picture captured the woman's reaction, a hearty laugh at whatever Liam whispered in her ear, his mouth so close to her neck. The other picture showed the same woman sprawled on a blanket, a magnolia blossom in her hair.

Brenawyn looked down at the corner of the photo for a digital date imprinted by the camera. Her mouth went dry. There had to be a mistake. The date read April 2011, more than two years after Brenawyn and Liam married.

Brenawyn covered the pictures, willing them to disappear. But now that she had seen them she had to look again, no matter how reluctantly. Almost blinded by tears, she uncovered them again to examine them and tried to determine the identity of the woman—no, she'd never seen her before. She wasn't some friend or acquaintance of theirs; they hadn't been taken at some innocent party or neighborhood get-together that Brenawyn could remember.

The way Liam, her husband, was looking at this blonde-haired woman was just…. Brenawyn threw the pictures in the trashcan beside the bed. *I won't even think about it. What good would it do? Rage at the possibility that Liam had an affair? Now, three years after he is gone? He never gave me any reason to doubt him.* Disgusted with herself she grabbed the can and tore into the trash; finding the glossy surfaces, she stormed out to the living room to dispose of them. She found a match, lit it and touched it to the photos, and after watching the flame take hold, tossed the pictures into the empty fireplace.

Ashes.

Appropriate.

She stormed away but returned just as quickly to watch the last of the embers wink out. She stood there

4

silently considering the incriminating, albeit circumstantial, evidence. "Ugh. Damn it!" She slammed her hand on the mantle. "Do you even know that he's dead?"

"Is everything a'richt, *a chuisle*?"

She turned to find Alex sitting in the leather wing chair in the shadowed recess of the room, book on his knee.

Brenawyn's breath hitched as she sighed. "Unpacking the last of the boxes from the house I shared with my husband." She glanced back at the fireplace, "I found some pic ... some unexpected things," she amended.

"Ah, lass, dae ye want ta talk about it?"

"No, thank you. I'd rather forget it all together."

A few steps into the hall took her back to the bedroom door where she stopped when she saw garbage strewn on the floor and her dog, Spencer, crouched in the corner, chewing a used tissue. "Spencer, put that down!" The dog bolted but Brenawyn wrestled him to the ground, prying his mouth open enough to extract his treat. "Mine!" She held the wet tissue aloft.

Sitting up, Brenawyn looked around her bedroom, now strewn with the contents of the remaining boxes from her former home.

Three years. Three years. If I close my eyes ... picking up the phone to hear ... seeing the wrecked guard rail, the car.... Ugh. Time doesn't heal shit.

Brenawyn reached over for the box of tissues on the nightstand and patted the bed beside her, "Come here, boy. Come on up."

She caught the eighty-pound bundle of wriggling fur. Not content with either licking her face or being as close to her as possible, Spencer did both simultaneously. "Eww, no doggie kisses." She scratched him under his collar. "Who's a good boy?" The dog tried one more time to sneak a last minute kiss that barely missed her open mouth, before giving up and settling down with a grunt as he nestled in, molding his body to her side. Absently she petted him, "You didn't know Liam. He was a good man, even though he was allergic to dogs."

The next item in the box was a small notebook filled with her husband's tight neat script. She leafed through it before recognizing what it was—the notebook that they shared when they took the philosophy class together during their last year of college. How she managed to get an A in the class was still a mystery to her when all she was concerned with was the heat of his body as he sat next to her.

She pulled out the insurance papers she had seen too often. "Again? How many copies did you keep? Did you think I would forget where they were?" she said aloud. She could almost hear his voice. *This is where copies of the insurance papers and the keys to the safety deposit box are*.... "How many times did we argue over this?"

Brenawyn dropped the papers, pushed the box across the bed, and flung herself back on it, startling the dog. She didn't move until she felt his wet nose nuzzle her arm. "It's okay, Spencer. Talking to you is one thing, but talking to the dead husband ... I need to stop that."

Resolved to finish, she picked up the box and

extracted the last item in the container, a small wooden box. Brenawyn ran her hand along the ornate brass fittings. Locked. She upended the box. No key. "Hmm." Running her hands along the back revealed a weak hinge. She tried prying the hinge with the edge of her fingernail, only to be thwarted when her nail broke. Sucking on the injured finger, she unfolded herself from the bed, climbed over the unmoving dog, and searched among the items strewn on the floor for the screwdriver she had seen earlier.

The hinges gave little resistance to the flathead screwdriver. Reaching in, Brenawyn took out a brightly wrapped gift box complete with a silver Mylar bow, flattened now after so long. She put the box on the nightstand, hesitant to open it. Liam had always been giving her surprise gifts. Packing his things away had been filled with the pain of finding boxes and gift bags he had obviously stowed away to give her at some future date. *Or had he meant them for that other woman?* The thought came unbidden to her mind, but she dismissed it quickly. It was unfair to Liam. It was just that it had been so long since the last time she stumbled upon a surprise like this from a man long dead.

~ ~ ~

Alex paced the room, but Brenawyn didn't return. Keeping an ear to the hallway, he strode over to the fireplace and sifted through the ashes. A soot-covered portion of a photo lay in the debris. Should he look at it? He hesitated. The photo had obviously disturbed Brenawyn. He didn't want to pry into her private life, but considering the dangers they still faced, it seemed necessary.

He stopped and plucked the photo from the fireplace, turning it over in his hand to see the two faces there. He drew a surprised breath. He should have expected this. Centuries may have passed, but Alex would always remember the face of James Morgan. Hatred boiled up from his gut; he needed to hit something.

He got some satisfaction as the brittle paper crumbled in his fist. He wished it were that easy. Jamie never gave him the opportunity. Coward.

I found some unexpected things. He paused. Was Jamie her husband? *Nay, it canna be*. She had always called him Liam. A common enough name: he had never connected it with James Liam Morgan McAllister.

Damn him.

He needed to hit something.

Always one step ahead.

A soft cry from the hallway pulled him back into the present and he flexed his clenched fist.

Alex stopped at the open doorway to see Brenawyn reaching for a wrapped gift on the nightstand. She fumbled with the paper, ripping at the seams with her teeth until the box was dented. She found purchase and wiped the bit of paper from her lip with one hand as the other pealed the paper away to reveal a black velvet jewelry box. Closing her eyes and holding her breath, she opened the box. He couldn't see what was inside but the facets of the stones spread sparkles across the ceiling as it caught the first rays of the day.

Brenawyn carefully removed the necklace and held it

up. Dangling the medallion from its chain as she approached the mirror, she traced the detailed design. She looped it around her neck, letting the medallion fall between her breasts.

"Years later I'm still finding stuff you left for me? This is why I couldn't live there anymore. I'm trying to move on with my life."

It was only then that she saw him in the doorway. She jumped. "Jesus, you scared me!"

"Lass, what's wrong? Is thaur anything I can dae ta help?"

"It's nothing." Sniffling and wiping her eyes with the back of her hand so hard that she saw spots. "My husband…," shaking her head, "my late husband would give me things, presents, jewelry and other pretty things." She carried the medallion to him, "Three years after his death, I am still finding gifts."

She dropped the necklace in his open hand and whirled to gather the rest of the items back into the box.

An exquisite medallion of gold Celtic knot work with ruby, sapphire, emerald, diamond, and topaz gemstones glinted up from his palm. He knew this necklace, could trace the pattern from memory if he needed more proof to convince him of what he already knew.

"T'is verra beautiful. It reminds me o' another. Come haur. Thaur is something…," Brenawyn straightened and met him, "I am curious about." He looped the necklace around her head, lifting her hair so the chain fell again her skin. He stepped back and looked unsatisfied, "The medallion needs ta be in contact with yer skin," and he went to make it so. Brenawyn pulled away blushing, his fingertip losing contact with her collar.

"Okay, I'll do it, thank you." And she dropped the medallion in her cleavage. "This is very strange. Necklaces are supposed to be worn outside…."

"Humor me." His face must have given something away because her eyes grew wide. "Turn around and leuk in the mirror."

Her reflection showed glowing sigils across her clavicle, dimming slightly across her shoulders to almost nothing as they tracked down her upper arms. He saw recognition reflected in her eyes. He knew she was remembering his explanation, "It is called Interlace; its path represents the thread o' life eternal, the crossings between the spiritual world o' Tir-Na-Nog and our own."

These were the same iridescent markings that were present after her recitation of the Lughnasadh thanksgiving incantation in Salem. Alex came up behind her and held her about the waist and the dimmed tracings burst to life, racing down her arms in matching intensity.

"What does this mean?" she asked as she searched his face reflected in the mirror.

"The necklace, or rather, the medallion, the chain, has nay power, is *Eiliminteach*—it means elemental. It is a mythic piece, one o' five, drenched in Druid lore. Five pieces, scattered, hidden, until the one is revealed. Foci most powerful for the priestess just as the torc is for the Shaman.

"Why are my markings activated by it? And why do they glow brighter at your touch?"

10

"The medallion is a sort o' antenna ta focus yer abilities." Eyes burning with desire, he swept aside her tresses and dipped his head so his lips brushed her ear. "My touch is different … are ya sure ye want ta ken, Brenawyn?"

She turned to face him and stepped back to look into his eyes, careful not to touch him.

"We are two halves ta a whole," he continued. "Shaman, priestess, man, woman, yin, yang, if ye will; we represent balance, and because o' that balance, the gods favor our union."

"If it is as you say, why would my husband have it amongst his belongings?"

Everything stopped as the weight of her words beat on his heart. "I ken yer husband a while sin." The words were out of his mouth before the decision to tell her registered in his mind. How he would explain his connection to James he had no clue. The truth? Hadn't she had enough of that?

Brenawyn looked at him, mouth agape. "How … how did you know Liam?"

"He never deserved yer loyalty. He wasna a kind man."

"What? You knew him?" Her arms uncrossed so that the robe gaped open. "When?"

"Brenawyn, I shouldnae ha' mentioned it. T'was a long time ago. Perhaps he changed."

"No. Tell me what he was like when you knew him. Please."

"T'was a long time ago. Please. Ye ha' good

memories o' him. Mine aren't so. I'd rather no' say."

She moved to bar the door, "No, damn it. Tell me."

"Liam and I were friends. I ken him as Jamie—James Liam Morgan McAllister. It doesna matter now. A woman came between us. We weren't friends any longer. End o' story." Alex brushed by her on his way out of the room, knowing that she was right on his heels.

"Your story lacks detail." Brenawyn caught his arm, "Please, tell me. It's been three years; I can't get over his death. My memories are fading but instead of making it better and allowing me to move on, I feel anxious and panicked, as if there is something important that I've forgotten, but I can't recall it."

"Brenawyn, if ye'll agree ta let it wait, I'll tell ye everything in time."

The back door opened with a squeak and Spencer bolted through the room, stepping on Brenawyn's bare foot. She hobbled, hopping on one foot; Alex grabbed her forearm to keep her from falling.

"Brenawyn, yer question, ask yerself this: why would he ha' the *Eiliminteach*?"

She stared at him for a moment before silently leaving the room.

Alex softly closed the door behind him, "Why, Jamie? Damn ye." He could have lived with the betrayal; eventually he would have stopped hating them so much if it had been true. Perhaps it was on her part. He'd never know after what Jamie had done to her. Now here he was centuries later with another woman whose memories were violated and altered by the same depraved animal.

12

Damn him.

All for power.

Not this time.

Alex would give Brenawyn the truth even if she hated him as a result.

Jamie—Liam was dead.

It was time the façade died too.

CHAPTER 2

LEO AVOIDED THE HOUSE—too many memories—but she loved the land. It called to her. The grove was a distance away from the house and the road beyond it, further out into the woods where she could shut out the human noises: a loud engine of some old jalopy wheezing by or what passed for music at an ear-bleeding decibel. When Tom had cleared the land—manually at her insistence—many of the oak and cedar trees had been young, but they flourished with more room to grow, their branches threading together over time. She added others over the years: a willow by the stream, then birch, elm, silver fir, rowan—more than she could remember. It was a peaceful, sacred place.

She placed the canvas bag in the center of the grove, taking out the ceramic bowl, a jar, and her mortar and pestle. She was unhurried in her preparations. Taking a knife, she went to the birch tree, peeling some of the exfoliating bark away. This was the first ingredient, appropriate for new beginnings and a cleansing of the past, something she should have done from the start. So much time had been wasted. If only she could go back … but that was a fool's dream. She knew why she had done it. She had made ignoring the obvious an art form. She had lived with the lie for so long that she had convinced herself that there was nothing otherworldly about Brenawyn.

She put the bark deep in her pocket and continued to the elm. She cut a low hanging branch, divested it of its leaves and placed it to join the birch bark. She looked at the tree. Funny how she took from it today as she had in the past: strength of will to save her unborn granddaughter so many years ago, and now that same strength of will to teach her granddaughter the fundamentals of Druidism today.

She walked to the oak and placed her palms against the wide strength of its trunk. She gazed above to its strong branches reaching out to the heavens above. The leaves rustled in the breeze, a few falling at the unseen mark of the coming of winter. She gathered her skirt and cut a piece of the bark, a piece of its armor to give strength and courage to what needed to be done.

She heard Alex approach. She was pretty sure this was intentional: he could move as silently as a wolf stalking its prey if he wanted to. He was coming to speak with her. Her mind was a jumble. She wanted him near so he could put himself in harm's way again to protect Brenawyn, repeatedly if necessary. But she wanted to drive him from her place, too. Willing the need for his protection away was not enough, though. She knew none of them could go back, so she had to come to terms with him and their situation, for which she had no one but herself to blame. Alex would take Brenawyn, and she would likely never see her granddaughter again.

Leo busily redoubled her efforts and she didn't look up, wanted to look absorbed, when he stopped in front of her. He stood there for what seemed to be an interminable time, but then sighed and lowered himself to sit opposite her on the grass. He held his side as he did; that caught her attention, and her eyes rocketed to his face.

"I'd have thought you wouldn't have pain?"

"I didna suppose ye ha' had much experience with bringing someone back from the deid?"

"I ... I don't."

"Just so then." Alex pressed his palm into his side and took a deep breath. "Thaur is always pain after. Doona be worrit for me, it will pass in time."

"How much time?"

"Ah, that depends on the extent o' the wounds. Normally, the pain would cripple a man new ta the resurrection process, but for yer intervention t'will cut down on recovery. I thank ye for that though t'was unnecessary, because my tolerance for pain is higher than that o' mortal men. I assure ye that I will be able ta defend against any that come for her."

"Like you did back in Salem?" Leo asked, disapproval clear in her voice.

"Aye. I ken that I let my guard down. T'was a

judgment call. I didna kin that Cormac would be so direct. That he would use the Oracle in such a direct way. They are desperate. They willna catch me off guard again."

Leo nodded, accepting his statement. "What's next?"

Alex looked at her grimly, saying nothing.

"How long do you think we have? How do we prepare?"

"A couple o' days a' the most ta be safe. We ought ta be gone long before he tracks us haur. If the Oracle got what she needs that willna even buy us that much time."

"I could run with Brenawyn and hide. There are places in the world we could do this. Places of extreme power to hide in plain sight as we did in Salem. We could go to New Orleans or Paris or Rome."

"Leoncha, even if t'were possible, how far do ye think ye would get? What was the toll on ye, Leo, for yer intercession with my resurrection?"

"How did you know?"

Alex touched the hair at her temples and untucked the lock behind her ear, rubbing the graying strands together to show her. "I ha' ne'er kent ye ta ha' gray in yer hair."

Leo took the hair from his opened hand and considered it.

"It happened almost immediately I would think," he added.

"Yes, and I, um, I have lost … I lost control."

"Control?"

She looked away and lowered her voice to a whisper, a tear running down her cheek, "My bladder…."

"Ah," he reached for her hand and gave it a squeeze,

17

"thaur is a cruel price ta pay, always. I ken o' what I speak."

"Yes, I'd assume you are well-versed in this area."

"Ye are no longer a young woman, and while ye are a strong healer, that's all ye are. Ye canna go up against the likes o' Cormac or the Vate. Ye doona ha' that kind o' power."

"The other option is unthinkable. To let her go, let you take her. The uncertainty will surely kill me."

Alex took a pen knife from his back pocket and opened his right hand to the sky, slicing across his palm. When enough blood welled in his cupped palm, he turned his wrist to let it drip on the ground. "I haurby gi' my blood oath ta protect…."

"Are you insane? Don't you realize what you are doing?"

"Aye, Leo. What else can I dae?"

"But, to take the blood oath alone? You'll be committing your soul."

"My soul?" Alex shook his head. "Leoncha, listen ta me: it doesna matter much what happens ta me; if she were ta die, or be seduced ta the Coven, all hope is lost. T'would destroy the balance, bring the Formor back ta this realm, and I didna kin what after that.

"But to bind yourself to her, you'll pine for her all the rest of your days."

"Dae ye love yer granddaughter so little then? Perhaps I ha' misunderstood. Can ye bare ta part with her knowing that ye canna protect her?

"Of course not!"

"Then let me, Leoncha. I am willing. I ken what a sacrifice yer making. Allow me ta promise all that I am ta dae that in yer place."

"But."

"No, Leo. I ha' already made up my mind. Ye canna stop me."

"You will become *Gancanagh* if she doesn't return your affection and take the oath herself. Your altruism will turn against you and transform you into a monster."

"I am already a monster."

"No, damn your eyes! Listen to me, Alexander Sinclair: you must not do this. You will fall into depravity. You'll lure innocents to crave your attentions."

Alex laughed at this, "In another context, ta tell a man that he'd have women begging, clamoring for his attentions, aye that would ha' been the devil's own temptation ta a much younger version o' myself." He grew sober, shaking his head slowly, "T'is all but done. Dae no' worry, Leoncha, I will fight the urge ta dae so when I become *Gancanagh.*" Alex looked up to the heavens, "Hear me. Hear me! All that I am, and all that I will be I pledge to Brenawyn McAllister, daughter of Margaret Farraday, granddaughter of Leoncha Callaghan. Furthermore, I haurby gi' my blood oath ta protect her as if she were my own. Her life is more sacred and more dear than my own, and if I am ta fail ta love and protect her, may I wander ceaselessly until the end o' time without the eternal reward."

Alex looked to Leo, "Say it."

"No. I won't."

"It canna be done until it is witnessed. Say it. Thaur is any other way."

Leo sighed, "Alexander Sinclair's vow was heard and acknowledged both in this world and beyond. With his word and mine, his fate is eternally sealed. So mote it be."

CHAPTER 3

He's out of the house for a bit. Went to the store. Only have a few minutes to write this down. It upsets him so when he sees me do this. Upset ... no, angry—he'll make me pay. So better to write when I'm alone.

My dreaming self remembers what my waking self does not.

I dream of patterns.

The triquetra—for the maiden, the matron, and the crone.

The triskele—for the sun, the afterlife, and the reincarnation.

The shield knot—for protection.

The tree of life—center for all.

The fivefold—for her who is to be.

I did not know what they were before.
My dreaming self has seen these symbols.
I did not know what they were before. Now, I wish I
knew not.
My dreaming self has seen them emblazoned
On my Brenawyn.

Brenawyn found her grandmother sitting at the kitchen table with Maggie. The nineteen-year-old had somehow found the time to change her hair color yet again. It now a bright blue. It was obvious that she and Leo were not just drinking coffee, but sharing secrets because when she walked in they shut their mouths and looked away suspiciously.

"Well," she said, crossing her arms across her chest and leaning on the door frame. "What are you two plotting?"

"Nothing, B. I was just asking about Alex. He's got the hots for you."

"Oh my God, Maggie! Shut up," she said, peeking down the hall. "He might hear you for God's sake. Keep your voice down."

"Not to worry," she said with a smirk. "He went out shortly after sunrise. I heard the screen door slam. He didn't say where he was going, but then again, I wasn't out here."

"All right, but, really, I feel awkward enough without your comments that could be overheard."

"I'm sorry, B. I won't mention it again, though you deserve to be happy."

"I know, sweetie, and I appreciate the sentiment, but

I am old enough to enter a relationship that doesn't involve my friend asking the man if he likes me. That's so high school."

Maggie chuckled chiding her, "Aren't you the one who says high school never ends?"

She came over and wrapped Brenawyn in a bear hug unbidden. As laborious as some of her childish antics were, Brenawyn had to remind herself that even though Maggie had to have the psychological fortitude of one much older to calmly accept all that happened within the last days, she still was only nineteen. She adapted to new information introduced by personal revelations and evidence of the existence of magic without a misstep. She was able to react without hesitation—the girl had one hell of a swing in the face of danger. Was it the fact that she was young still that allowed her to acclimate so easily? Or was it something else? Brenawyn realized beyond knowing the tragic details of her life: deadbeat father, abusive boyfriend, she really didn't know the mettle of this girl she considered her little sister.

Brenawyn steeled her face as Maggie pulled away. There wasn't time to delve into what motivated her. Though Brenawyn couldn't define it further, she felt the building anxiety of a deadline with each passing hour. She stepped away and surreptitiously watched as Maggie hooked the leash onto Spencer's collar before walking out the back door. She strangely felt the need to spend as much time with her as possible, almost as if she was never going to see her again—which of course, was impossible. She couldn't think of anything that would take her away, though try as she might, Brenawyn couldn't shake the feeling.

Putting the coffee cup down, her grandmother folded her hands in front on the table and looked her in the eye. "Yes? What is it, Pussy Cat?"

Brenawyn stared out the back door for moments after the storm door clicked shut and she couldn't see their combined shadow any longer before turning the kitchen chair to face her grandmother. "All right, I have some questions." She ignored the implicit unasked question her grandmother posed unready for the conversation that would ensue.

"I was reading some of Mom's journal, and one entry made mention of the patterns," Brenawyn rubbed her arm absentmindedly where the interlace had appeared, not just when Alex had put the medallion around her neck but at other times, too; when she had saved her dog Spencer from a vicious attack by the Order, when she had called upon the spirits at the Lughnasadh ceremony in Salem a few weeks before. "But she didn't mention the colors, at least not in what I've read so far. Do you know anything about it?"

Leo took off her cardigan, and gently folded it, placing it on the table next to her. She sat back in the chair and inhaled deeply. The interlace flared to life, originating under her sleeveless cotton shell it raced outward to cover her clavicle and neck in one direction and her bare arms and hands in the other.

The hairs on Brenawyn's arms stood on end.

"The symbols are a blessing from the gods, and each

24

color represents an ability. Mine are blue, which represents the healing of water, washing away imperfection, disease, infection. My abilities lie in the healing arts. Alexander's blue means the same, but his sigils are mostly red. Red is for defense. His caste is that of the warrior. Not an original caste, but one derived from necessity. Many over the centuries craved our power; others feared it, wanting to wipe us out of existence, particularly the Romans. That's about the time when the warrior caste emerged."

"So what do green, gold, and silver mean?" she asked, rubbing her arm lightly.

Her grandmother took her hand, "Activate your sigils, Pussy Cat, like I taught you."

Brenawyn closed her eyes and concentrated. She wasn't all that confident she'd be able to conjure them if she was alone, but while touching, holding her grandmother's hand, feeling the resonation with her, then yes, she could call her interlace. She could feel its warmth as it radiated outward from her chest, though the pat on the back of the hand by her grandmother was added confirmation that the patterns could now be clearly seen.

Leo traced the pattern up Brenawyn's arm, slightly tickling her as she moved from Brenawyn's wrist to her shoulder.

"Green is life. A strong connection to the Earth. The Earth will respond to you. The animals will listen. But you know that. You've always had a way with animals."

She lifted her fingers to resume on a different part of the exposed skin. "Silver and gold are for clergy, high priestesses only. Gold is associated with the sun, and silver the moon, both are integral parts of each other. The sun represents the gods in the spirit realm, the moon, the ability to speak to them."

"My skin, it glows."

"The five colors."

"Does it mean … "

"Yes?"

Brenawyn shook her head, "I don't know. But I didn't have this all my life."

"No. You didn't—you wouldn't. Years of training would develop the abilities, but if none were received, it would wither away. Although sometimes, even without training, the interlace will manifest itself after periods of sustained grief or trauma."

"Grief or trauma, like Liam's death?"

"That could have done it, but it didn't trigger it."

"So why now? What was so special about the events we just lived through, being accosted in the bathroom, the ceremony, attacked in your backyard, and Spencer … "

"Well, let's look at it in reverse. Your powers were already manifesting by the time Spencer was stabbed," said Leo, referring to the attack by the Order on Brenawyn in the backyard of her grandmother's shop in Salem which had occurred a few weeks before. Spencer had gallantly defended her from the attacker, but had been stabbed in the process.

"Your interlace allowed you to save him, even though you were not trained in healing. It was no random attack. That man was coming for you, so the interlace had manifested enough for the Oracle to have a vision of you,"

Leo explained. "The Lughnasadh ceremony, I suspect, is when it happened. By offering to take my place because I had injured my leg, the pantheon saw you as their willing participant. That is the first requirement from officiant to sacrifice, whether temporary or permanent."

Brenawyn thought about what her grandmother had just said and nodded. Her memories of the Lughnasadh ceremony were hazy; she had been possessed by the spirit of Aine, the goddess of fertility. Even though her memories weren't clear, her face grew red at the thought of the steamy interlude with Alex that had followed the ceremony, and she quickly changed the subject.

"What of visions and omens?"

"You should know better, Brenawyn, than to ask that. Is it so different than Catholicism that people have visions? It is written in the Bible on several occasions."

"That's true."

"And as far as omens go, people have always tried to interpret meaning from their environment. Is it so farfetched to try to determine when it's going to rain, or if the storm will be a severe one? I mean, the method may seem odd, watching for changes in animal behavior, but animals are more sensitive to things like that."

"Now that you mention it, I think there were studies done on horses being able to predict earthquakes."

"See, not so weird."

"But some methods are extreme. Do not tell me you hold with evisceration as a means of prediction?" Her pointed question brought up vivid scenes of horror. Though she hadn't seen Barbara's body herself, the kindly bakery owner across the street from her grandmother's place, the scene had been described to her in minute detail by the police the night of her murder. That, combined with the blood stained cobblestones left after the crime scene had been fully processed, left her with night terrors. If imagination was a poor substitute for actual sight, she'd rather stick to imagination for it filled in the gaps of what was a drawn-out, grisly death.

Barbara had been killed by the Vate to help the Order locate Brenawyn. Brenawyn, despite all she had seen in the past few weeks, was still finding it difficult to accept that her twenty-eight years of living in a normal, fact-based, scientific world were at an end; that she now lived in a world where gods and goddesses and magic were real, and that she was some kind of reincarnation of a long-lost high priestess.

"Brenawyn, honey, look at me. I know what you're thinking. Don't go there. You'll just be beating yourself up trying to make sense of her death. To these people, her life meant nothing. There is no reason. They will stop at nothing to get to you. As for your question, no, of course I don't hold with it. But these people do very much believe in it and you have to accept that so you can ward yourself against it."

Brenawyn stifled back tears and nodded her head.

"It is an ancient custom. Back then, you have to understand, it was a different time, savage, harrowing, people unsure of where the next threat would originate. I can understand why they did anything they could to gain some information on what the future might hold for them.

They were trying to carve out an existence, some stability and surety in a time when nothing was constant. Blood offerings do offer some clarity; they just don't have to be as vicious as what was done to Barbara."

She opened her hands and showed them to Brenawyn, a scabbed over slice to the meaty part of her palm showed red. "Why do you think my hands are so scarred?"

Tears welled in Brenawyn's eyes as she took her grandmother's hand and covered it with her own, "When did you do this?"

"The night that Barbara was murdered. Alex asked me to scry for a location of the Oracle."

"And what did it do?"

"Visions are like dreams. They don't adhere to the linear. They are illogical and are often full of symbols. The blood is like wearing goggles when you swim underwater in the ocean. It makes things clearer; there is still the murk to wade through, but it makes it much less disorienting."

"Is it just human blood that makes things clearer?"

"In ancient times animal blood was used more frequently, but it depended on the situation and what vision the seer was seeking. I've used animal blood.

"Ugh. Nana! But why?"

"Listen Brenawyn, I didn't go out to slaughter an animal for the sole purpose of using its blood in a ritual. You seem to forget I was a farmer's wife. If we wanted to eat, we had to kill the chicken or lamb. That's the truth of it. We have moved so far away from the way things were. You go to the grocery store to buy chicken cutlets, but do you ever think of how those cutlets got there? Someone had to kill the chicken, cut it up, package it, and send it to the store. Don't look at me with that disgust on your face," Leo said indignantly.

"I'm sorry, Nana."

"It's okay. Mine is not the first religion to do this. There are Old Testament stories that refer to acts of sacrifice, but little thought is given to how things must have been. Animals were scarce and expensive. If a sacrifice was to be made, the people sacrificed according to their beliefs, but likely retained the meat to feed themselves and only sacrificed the inedible. Greek and Roman accounts made mention of this too."

"Will I be expected to … ?"

"I think you know the answer to that already, but we're a long way from that. I think we got off track here."

Brenawyn nodded, took a breath, and said, "So, willingness is the first requirement. What is the second? How many others are there?"

"The second is precision. You took the time to study the ritual; you said the proper words giving thanks to all the gods. How did you prepare?"

"I heard you practice it so many times, saw you perform it for years."

"Nothing else?"

"No, not that I can remember … wait."

"What?"

"Wait, wait. Let me think." Brenawyn got up from the table and paced away, muttering to herself.

"Your grandfather did that."

Brenawyn looked up, "Huh?"

"He mumbled to himself when he was thinking about something important. You reminded me of him just now."

She smiled. "Nana, do you remember the night you told me that you were a Druid? A few days before the ceremony? I stormed out of the house to clear my head."

"I remember."

"Well, I ran into Alex and we ended up taking a walk to the ceremonial grounds. He was telling me stories about the ritual and what the officiant would do the night before."

"Ah, did it have something to do with asking permission?"

"Yes, that was it."

Leo nodded her head, "The picture is becoming clearer. Did you by chance ask permission?"

"Ugh, yes, I didn't know what I was doing. I was so swept up in the story, that I didn't even think that in so doing it might be seen as disrespectful."

"Well, now it makes more sense that your latent abilities were activated by the thanksgiving ceremony. Brenawyn, would you do me a favor? Really think about this before you make a decision. Your life has become more complicated and dangerous, but I think it's manageable yet. If you choose this you will own the danger. Choosing this lifestyle, you will be trained to use your magic and will be able to defend yourself. But make no mistake, if you accept this destiny, they will come for you, and there will be no going back."

"So, no pressure then. Thanks."

"Brenawyn. Just think about it. Please. Spend some

time with Alexander. He knows all of the history; he can teach you the basics before you have to decide anything."

"Speaking of Alexander. He's a history professor, a priest, an occult connoisseur, a magic man and a werewolf?"

"A werewolf! Don't be ridiculous. He's a shape-shifter."

"Oh, that clears everything up then."

"Brenawyn, he's the Shaman—a teacher and defender of the Old Ways."

"The same Shaman that would have sex with the high priestess on Beltaine, to what—represent the fertility of the Earth? I'm supposed to be this high priestess? So, are you telling me that we are, what, fated to fall in love or something?

"Not that he's decrepit and has leprosy or anything, he's rather, well ... extremely handsome, but really! You're my grandmother for God's sake. Aren't you supposed to be guarding my virtue or something?"

"I am so glad I rate so high in yer esteem, Brenawyn."

She turned to find Alexander standing directly behind her. Where had he come from? How had he approached so silently? Shit, why was he always here whenever she turned around? She felt the color creep up her neck, abashed, "I didn't mean ... I don't think of you ... I, I, I know I asked ... well I don't know what to think. Excuse me." She brushed by him as if on a mission, wishing that she was back in Jersey, in her house. Life was so simple, so ordinary then.

She headed for her bedroom and softly clicked the

door closed, although she wanted to slam it repeatedly to clear some frustration. She thought better of it, slamming the door was childish. Where was the dog? Oh, Maggie had him. Figures, just when she needed some canine comfort. Spencer didn't want to turn her world upside down; he didn't want her to discard her faith for a new one, so strangely different. He didn't ask anything of her besides a belly rub and some doggie treats.

She flopped on the bed and crammed the sham under her chin. She lay like this for a while, looking at the pattern of the headboard's wood grain but not seeing it. She sighed and turned her head to face the nightstand, the blue cloth of her mother's journal stood out as a beacon. *Perhaps, I can get some comfort from Mom.* She reached for the journal and opened to a random page in the middle of the book.

August, 1982

Awake with a start. Smoke? Yanked forcibly from bed. Rescued? No ... captured. No sense. Why wasn't it making any sense? Hands like vices held my arms pinned to my sides as unseen faces shoved and pinched. Fighting and trying to protect my swollen stomach, I didn't try to fend off the punches that landed anywhere else. Tears streaming down my face as punches rained down on my head. Off balance and unprepared for the boot to the lower back, I found myself sprawled over the front threshold landing on my hands and knees in the mud. Peering over my shoulder struggling to see past the massed bodies, I could just see the newly carved trundle splintered, pieces strewn across the floor through the small space of the common room. Searching hopelessly around for help, flames licked at the edges of the curtains. The house was gone. Several men nearby tossed their torches onto the thatched roof. Thrust to my feet and dragged away, just before the cloth bag covered my face, the roof smoldered for endless moments and then in a big whoosh, it was consumed.

Lost to the passage of time, was today the third day or just the second? The clouds were a lighter gray interspersed at times with clear blue sky, even though it was still misting. I could hear the morning stirring of my neighbors; the jingle of a horse's bridle and clop of its hooves as it passed, the clatter of shutters thrown open, soon a new volley of taunts and missiles would be sent my way.

Mud-splattered and chilled to the bone, I hugged the wall in a vain attempt to get some protection from the icy rain as it continued to patter down. Exposure allowed my gore to settle and with pity I observed the worms leach from the walls of the prison only to plop into a watery grave. I bent down to scoop up a worm from the nearly shin deep water and stuffed it in my mouth, barely chewing. I gagged but fought the reflex to vomit by quickly swallowing. I would be damned if I would eat the filth that had been thrown upon me. Stale and moldy bread, meat infested with maggots—fare not even fit for vermin. Worms were more appetizing given the options. I had to remain strong if for only a little while to see.

The first of my tormentors for the day arrived shortly

after, a group of children. The children were the worst, fed lies and superstitions by their ignorant parents from birth; they knew no better and were merciless. Thinking of new forms of torment, these children, who I could picture in my mind because I knew each of them, threw a live snake into the pit with me. They laughed maniacally as I splashed to get away from it. I dug at the walls pulling at errant roots trying to climb above the water level. The roots gave and the rain-softened earth offered no holds as it oozed between my fingers. I turned, armed with a sharp stone I had dislodged, desperately trying to locate the serpent in the gloom. In one motion I pounced on it, finding myself on my knees in the muck grasping the writhing snake in my hand; I bashed it repeatedly until it no longer struggled. Screaming obscenities, I stood shakily and flung the bloody remains away from me.

August 23, 1982

He tells me that he found me out in the garden, mud stained and drenched, scribbling in my journal. He tells me it was a dream.

It was just a dream.
A nightmare.
But why I can still taste the worm?

September 15, 1982

I sleep alone now locked in our bedroom. The bolt he installed himself on the outside. Every time that bolt slides home, a little more of my hope dies with it.

CHAPTER 4

Brenawyn looked around room; the door was closed, and all she could think of was to get out. She needed to get away. She cracked the door and listened, no sound, good to slip out unnoticed. She tied her hikers on and with a glimpse down the hallway skirted out, only to find Alexander and her grandmother huddled in the corner whispering.

Her curiosity was peaked, but she had too much pride to ask what they were talking about, even though she was very sure it had something to do with her. Instead she announced, "I'm going out."

Alexander looked up. "Wait, lass. We ha' found another bundle, the same that I burned at the Salem house." He offered it for Brenawyn to see.

"So?"

"T'was amongst yer effects haur in the attic. T'is

meant for ye."

"I don't want it."

"Ye doona ken, lass. This is a memory binding. This is the second o' three."

"I'm still not following."

"Brenawyn, right now, tell me about yer husband."

Looking askance at him, "Why?"

"A happy memory. Detailed."

"Um, let's see, there was the time he took me to see a play—what was it? It was … hmm? That's funny."

"What is?"

"I can't recall it."

"Just as I thought."

"What? Just as you thought about what? Because I can't remember the name of the play? You asked me out of the blue. That's why I can't remember. It would be like I asked you to say something funny. You wouldn't be able to do it."

"A'richt, but humor me for a minute." Alex strode passed her and into the kitchen, Nana following on his heels. "Sit down, Brenawyn. Leo, stay by her just in case."

He pulled a copper pot off the overhead rack placing it on the stovetop with a bang. A lit match was introduced to the dried twigs of the sachet and thrown into the pot. The bits caught instantly, that same strange smell pervading the room. Once the smell was in her nostrils, *she was back in Salem prying the first bundle from Spencer's jaws on the staircase. Feeling the saliva-wet velvet bag, loosening its strings, and pouring out the dried herbs into her hand.* Alex knew what it was then too, as he snatched

37

it from her. His reaction was the same as it was now, to burn the sachet.

It was too much to bear. Brenawyn could feel tension behind her eyes build, the onset of a headache. She pinched the bridge of her nose, massaging the area above futilely to try to relieve the pressure. "Put yer head down, but continue ta breathe, Brenawyn. Help her, Leo."

The intensity of the headache increased so the fading light of the setting sun burned her eyes and the overhead lights felt as if they pounded on her head. Brenawyn gave in; the tabletop looked like a welcome place, at least a place to keep her head from rolling off her shoulders.

I woke with a start back in my bedroom, the coverlet and sheets twisted in knots around my legs. Sweat drenched my body, but my hands went automatically to my swollen belly. A healthy kick answered back. I smiled.

The movement made getting up a necessity so I shuffled out of bed, and padded down to the bathroom. My back was turned to Liam, when he called out. I turned as I reached the bathroom door. The smile on my face disappeared when I saw the scowl on his. "

"What did I tell you about making the bed as soon as you get up?"

"I was just going to the bathroom; the baby is ... "

He ran his hands through his hair, and grunted. "It's always the baby. I'm tired of you using him as an excuse to be lazy."

"Liam, Please. I'll make the bed just let me go ... "

He hesitated for a moment, but the decision was visible on his face as soon as he made it. It happened so quickly, he turned and punched the wall bellowing, and stalked down the hall to me grabbing my arm painfully. "No. You will do it now!"

I cringed, covering my stomach with my free hand, and tried to pull away to retreat into the safety of the bathroom, "Please, I have to go."

He pulled me along, urine trickled down my legs. Panic set in. It would make him angrier. I tried to stop it, but only succeeded in resisting his pull. He turned on me, nostrils flaring, and looked down. I tried to hide it, tried to cover the wetness, but he saw.

He turned up his nose in disgust, and yanked on my arm.

"Please, you're hurting me."

"Stop it, bitch!"

"Please, you'll hurt the baby!"

"And if I do, it will be your fault. Now get in there!"

He stepped on the toe of my worn out sock when he pivoted me around him. I stumbled and suddenly, I was free of Liam's punishing grip. I reached out to the railing—

Brenawyn opened her eyes despite the searing headache, heaved, and vomited on her grandmother's kitchen floor. She shook from the exertion and the fragmented memory. The pounding started to lessen and she slumped boneless to the table, silently wracked by sobs.

Gentle hands were rubbing her back; strong arms lifted her from the chair, over her mess and carried her into the dim living room to be wrapped in the crocheted afghan cuddled into the corner of the couch.

Alex moved the coffee table and knelt in front of her. Her grandmother hovered nearby.

"*A chuisle*, tell me, what are ye remembering?"

Brenawyn clamped her lips shut and shook her head.

"T'would be better if ye told us."

She shook her head again, tears spilling over, and wrapped her arms about herself, rocking back and forth.

Alex sat next to her and tried to gather her in his arms. She stiffened. She didn't want to be touched. How could it be possible? She had never been pregnant. How could she have been? She would remember. How could she forget? How could she know what it felt like? Doubt. Was this what insanity feels like? Her heart pounded in her chest. Her mind raced, screamed at her to run, to get away from him, from here. Her mind rebelled at what her gut was telling her was true. The memory of the living heaviness, both foreign and home simultaneously, the secret butterflies, and early movement almost undetectable, the pressure that almost tickled, only for the briefest of times. Secret shared moments between mother and child. She wanted to scream. She wanted to hit something. She wanted to hurt. How could she forget! How could she forget?

She felt Alex reposition himself and try to pull her close, offering comfort. He must have felt the change in her. She resisted. There was no comfort he could give her. She didn't deserve any. She had forgotten about her child—her son. Her son! What—where was he? What had happened? But her gut told her she knew already.

40

Leo finally, put her hand on his arm, "Let me."

Alex looked up at Leo, and back at Brenawyn, before making a move off the couch. At his movement she pulled further away from him, pressing herself awkwardly into the cushions shaking, her head coming to rest as she stared at the ceiling.

"Go. Let us just sit awhile."

"We canna leave her like this, Leoncha. Two o' the bindings are destroyed, but likely, the third is no' haur. I ha' ta bring her to Tir-Na-Nog for the goddess ta release her mind."

"You cannot do it here?"

"Aye," Alex paced away, but returning quickly, shaking his head. "Nay, I canna. I doona ken enough about the original spell ta safely remove the rest. I'd just as likely make her permanently daft."

"Then go and prepare."

Alex glanced back to see Brenawyn crumble into the arms of her grandmother.

CHAPTER 5

Before dawn Leo awoke in the living room next to the sleeping form of her granddaughter whose tear-streaked face was nuzzled into a crocheted baby blanket. Leo moved and her joints protested. A white hot pain shot up her neck behind her ear, quick movement remonstrated by her stiff neck. She ushered on, using it to fuel her anger. The second memory binding was found and destroyed and with it all peace of mind for her, and most of all for poor Brenawyn. A spell to wipe all memory of Brenawyn's son. What was the fucking purpose? The only ones who could work such an intricate spell, one that would be so all encompassing, branching out to include multiple people, would be the gods whom she worshipped. Why? She was caught between Scylla and Charybdis, having no preferable options. She couldn't leave Brenawyn as she was with one remaining binding out there. She'd go crazy, castigating herself for perceived shortcomings. She would never feel as if she was worthy of anything good, haunted by the half memories of forgetting about her child.

How does a mother come back from that? She wouldn't be able to offer any solace. Losing a child like she herself had was nothing like Brenawyn's situation. Leo wanted to rant and rail at the gods; their manipulations an effrontery that could not, would not, be tolerated any longer! It would do no good though, with the last of the bindings out of reach, the only ones that could offer some release *would be* the gods. The destruction of the spell in total was the only way that Brenawyn could find some semblance of peace of mind. At least she would know the whole truth, and perhaps that, in some small, infinitesimal way, would offer release of guilt. Was that small hope enough to send Brenawyn away from all the support she had in Leo, Maggie, and even the dog, probably forever?

She knew what Alexander would say. His purpose had been clear from the start. He needed Brenawyn, willing or not, to return as the living symbol of the Accords to be the arbiter of a more lasting peace between ancient forces. He had pledged himself to Brenawyn risking everything of himself, but he was still extrinsically motivated. Truth be told, Leo was angry at him too. He was the Shaman; he should be enough to hold the balance. After all he was the Reliquary, the physical embodiment of the entire history of the Druids. He had knowledge of what came before and some semblance of what would be. He could conduct himself as he saw fit to ensure that balance was maintained and harmony preserved. Leo ultimately didn't care about him; she admired him, loved him perhaps, but he was not her own.

She knew what she had to do, and it made her sick. For the sake of any hope, however slim, of Brenawyn's state of mind, Leo would say goodbye to her granddaughter, and let Alex take her to the gods to restore her memories. From there, Brenawyn's fate was completely out of her hands. Leo wouldn't be there to offer her assistance or guidance, Brenawyn would be operating from within a nest of vipers. Would Alex's guidance be enough to ward her away from becoming beholden to the gods? Would his lessons be enough for her to hold her own burgeoning abilities? Would his protection be enough to quell the power play from the Coven?

These questions remained unanswered.

Brenawyn stirred on the couch, nuzzling in the blanket. Leo reached down and brushed the hair off her forehead, and she started at the sudden touch. Leo smiled, "When you are ready, I want you to meet me in the back."

Brenawyn sniffled and moved to sit up, tucking the afghan under her arms, and nodded.

A half hour later in the backyard, Leo heard Brenawyn approach, and turned to greet her with a smile. "Take the knife and cut a branch from the holly, apple, and willow, Pussy Cat."

Brenawyn stepped into the circle, a small sad smile on her lips "It's more beautiful than I remembered." She crossed the grove, placed a kiss on her grandmother's cheek, and did as she was instructed. Leo sat on her knees in the middle of the circle adding the contents of her pocket to the ceramic basin. She was careful to shred the birch bark into pieces over the elm and oak so the sparks would be sure to catch. A mindless task, perfect to ready herself for meditation.

She was showering the collection with sparks from the flint when Brenawyn knelt down, her hands full of the branches she had been assigned to get. "Take the leaves off each branch but keep them separate. I'll tell you when to add them."

"Wouldn't it be easier just to use a match?"

"Easier, yes, but it wouldn't meet the same results. Be patient."

A fire slowly caught with the added measure of lightly blowing on the pile. "There. A fire." Pleased with herself, Leo sat back and stared at Brenawyn. She had her lips upturned at the corner showing amusement at the situation but she sat patiently, meeting Leo's eyes and looking away intermittently.

Leo sighed. "Lesson three, or perhaps its four. Whatever, it doesn't matter. The trees. The trees around you are each significant to the Druid religion. I have burning here," indicating with a swish of her hand, "birch, elm, and oak, all of which represent strength in some way. This is my contribution to the workings of the meditation spell." She scooched over and touched the apple branch which was devoid of leaves, "The branch from the apple tree."

"It means knowledge."

"The fruit, yes, but the branch means more: youth, beauty, happiness, immortality. It's the immortality that we want here, the immortality of faith. Even if there is only one person who believes, doctrine lives on."

Leo moved to touch the next pile. "The willow represents healing and magic. I know you don't believe in magic … "

"There is no such thing," Brenawyn cut in.

"Well, think of it as miracles instead," Leo replied patiently. "Miracles or magic happen all around us, sometimes it takes a careful eye to pick them out. Bad things happen also, but that does not mean there is no such thing as a miracle. You can call it magic that you weren't hurt by your attacker, or you can call it a miracle. Was it magic or a miracle that your pup lived after being stabbed?"

"What was it when I lost my child?" Tears spilled, "that I so easily forgot his existence?"

"Brenawyn … " Leo was at a loss of words. Nothing she knew could ease her pain.

But it was Brenawyn who spoke next, "But I guess you're right. So, what's the last represent?"

"Then finally, we have the holly branch. The leaves are hard and spined. It represents a warrior, but of the spiritual kind. Put them in the fire, starting with the apple, then holly, followed up by the willow. That's it," she added as Brenawyn carefully placed the branches on the fire. "All right, once you get the hang of it, you won't need the words, but for now you can use mine. Repeat after me.

"I come in search of peace."

"I come in search of peace," Brenawyn repeated each line after her grandmother.

"In the name of the Crone, who guides my wisdom.
"In the name of the Mother, who gave me birth.
"In the name of the Maiden who will cherish me.
"I seek the passion of the Lady.
"I seek the wisdom of the Lady.
"I seek the magic of the Lady.
"I seek the blessings of the Lady.
"With the grace of three granted
"Let me find peace."

"Let me find peace," Brenawyn sobbed. The comforting silence enveloped Brenawyn and Leo, blocking the extraneous noises from the surrounding wood. Leo could see the shock on Brenawyn's face as the veil closed around her. She swung her head to scan the trees, saw the birds still there, the squirrels skittering up one tree and down the next but no sound came from it. She turned to Leo, who sat patiently waiting for Brenawyn to settle her thoughts.

It was a shock the first time, Leo knew. Once it grew comfortable, the purpose of the meditation spell became obvious, it blocked all distraction. Except questions looked as if they would spill from Brenawyn's lips, but with a shake of her head, Leo closed her eyes and hopefully put to rest any question that would bubble over. She sat that way for a time, relishing the silence. She let the general worries of life fade away. Uncertainties about the shop and financial matters, they always seemed to work themselves out. The deeper concerns were harder to let go, such as mourning for Thomas. She always thought she would go first. How would he have handled things?

And then Margaret. A mother shouldn't outlive her children.

They were both gone, too long now.

Then there was Brenawyn. Gods, how was she to help her? Losing her parents, her baby, even her husband—that bastard. Having every belief she had turned upside down, having her faith tested, shattered. Uncertainty twisted its way in to her thoughts. Why was she doing this again? She should take Brenawyn and run. Stay hidden, though where would they go? The anonymity of a city? New Orleans. Hiding in plain sight again, but there was so much power in that city. Alex was right, she wasn't strong enough to fend off attacks and she wouldn't even know they were coming, in the midst of all that raw power.

"Brenawyn is vulnerable, with powers just coming to light now, she can be manipulated and honed as a weapon or stripped of them completely and probably killed like Barbara," Leo thought.

It was this last thought that solidified her resolve.

She long since had memorized Brenawyn's face. She missed those long years watching the subtle changes, as she grew from the chubby roundness of the infant to the emergence of her personality as a toddler to the bones growing in adolescence to reveal the lines of what she would look like as an adult. Damn her stubborn father. Too many years wasted.

But that was the past. The question was what to do in the present. Perhaps she should drive Brenawyn away, let Alexander protect her. He would, with his very life, she knew. Brenawyn would have to believe her. God, she'd seen enough to believe already, but still she clung to her rational world, trying as hard as she could to ignore the magic all around her. If Alex shifting from wolf to man and back again in front of her in Salem wasn't enough, if assisting in bringing him back to life him back to life wasn't enough, what would it take? Brenawyn had enough proof.

Yes, Leo would start as soon as the meditation was over. *Yes, that's it. I'll explain the whole truth to her. After I do, there will be no turning back.* Of course, that meant that Brenawyn would have to leave. She'd have to talk to Alex first, find out his plans. Did he want to do the rite here? There were the falls not too far off, though water underground was preferable. The nearby caverns were perfect, but an impossibility. They were locked up tight after hours. Perhaps, he'd want to travel to Scotland; she could go with them if that were the case. Spend some more time with Bren before …

Leo studied Brenawyn. The sweep of her lashes lay against her flushed cheeks covering bright eyes alive with activity, a slight smile played on her lips. Brenawyn smiled more fully at the light breeze and with a sigh crumpled to the ground, runes glowing lightly under her skin. Leo was at her side instantly; turning her over she found pulse and heartbeat strong, counter-indicating a faint. What was wrong?

"Brenawyn, honey. Wake up. Please." No response.

Should she leave to go get help? Did Brenawyn have her cell phone? Rummaging in her granddaughter's pockets revealed the small device. No reception. She threw it on the ground and took Brenawyn by the arms and shook her. "Wake up. I can't carry you back and I don't what to leave you alone."

A voice boomed out, "Doona try ta wake her."

Turning, she saw Alexander at the far perimeter of the circle. "You scared me." Leo looked at the surrounding landscape; even though it was only the eve of summer, a thick blanket of dried foliage covered the ground, "I didn't hear you." Looking down, "Help me carry her to the house."

Alexander approached to take a knee by Brenawyn's head, "Nay. She canna be moved. T'would cause too much disorientation. Best ta wait haur." Alex sat down in the grass and answered the look on Leo's face. "Yer granddaughter has crossed over."

"What? To Tir-Na-Nog? Impossible. That takes years of training. Even I have never been able to do it."

"Leo, dae we ha' ta ha' this conversation again?"

"Yes, damn it. Damn you. Yes, we do."

Sighing, he began, "Ye are a devote practitioner and ye ha' developed yer abilities ta be a formidable threat if necessary, but those abilities … I'm sairy, but those abilities are limited. They fall short o' being able ta cross realms."

Leo sighed and wiped her eyes. "Then you'll go? Go to her? You'll take her now?"

"Aye. I will. And when we get back … "

"Everything will be different."

"Leoncha. I want ye ta go ta the house. Find Maggie if ye can ta help ye. When Brenawyn is free o' the last binding, the memories will come flooding back."

"Yes, I'll be here waiting for her. I'll be prepared."

"Nay, ye doona kin what that will mean for ye. Her memory and yers are tied. Ye had nay recollection o' the bairn she carried. That's why I wouldna try ta undo it. Ken? Normally, the focus o' the bindings is only one. This one, howe'er, is nothing like I ha' e'er seen. Only the God of Memory could ha' weaved it."

"I surmised as much, but to what end?"

"Ha' ye e'er been able ta ken why the gods act as they do, woman? I ha' been on this earth far longer than ye, and I ha' nay clue. They use us; manipulate us like pawns on a chess board for their own amusement."

Leo looked at Brenawyn's prone body for a long moment, "Do you trust Oghma that far?"

"Trust one o' the Sidhe at yer own peril, but with this, aye, I'll ha' ta."

Leo took a long intake of breath, and whispered, "Then go."

~ ~ ~

The warm breeze welcomed him to Tir-Na-Nog. Alex looked around expectantly for Brenawyn, but was met only by the lonely expanse of the plain before the forest. Before he turned to break the connection, to traverse the rift again in reverse to return to the world where Brenawyn, just a lovely woman, waited, he saw a flutter of purple by the tree line. Brenawyn was looking up into the treetops. She reached out to touch and everything stopped, frozen in place. He gained her position and she looked at him questioningly. "What is this place?"

"T'is called Tir-Na-Nog."

"Tir-Na-Nog." She tried the pronunciation on her lips. "I have been here before."

He nodded, but said nothing. He could feel the weight of her stare but he refused to meet her eyes. "We ha' a ways ta travel. Ye can ask questions on the way."

Alex walked in silence, letting Brenawyn take it all in. He remembered his first time here, though this would be her second? Well, regardless, this was the first time she knew where she was—overwhelming to say the least. The blades of grass caressed her legs as they passed. Curious, she reached down and sure enough, the blades swayed against her hands. She touched a tree and the bark undulated, surprising her. "What?"

"The trees, the grass, everything is a collection o' smaller beings. The trees and grass, and everything ye see are forest dryads. Divine in nature, but with verra specialized powers. Haur, they are small ta make the whole. Thaur, they are... bigger ta start with, but they ha' corporeal bodies and a mischievous mind. The world has nay way ta define them as one o' many, so they are forever vying for time thaur. Mischievous, because ta their minds, they havena long, time passes differently haur. I suppose e'ery being wants individuality e'en when they see the importance o' being part o' something bigger."

Brenawyn touched the tree's bark again, running her hand along it, watching intently the reaction. She looked to him, smiling, and moved to the next tree, then rock, then flower. She paused at this, growing very still. She scanned the surrounding forest, unsure of herself. She saw movement and her body tensed and shifted to a crouch. She motioned for him to do the same, but Alex didn't move. She must have sensed his inaction because she threw a look over her shoulder to find him standing patiently, hands clasped behind his back. "Nothing haur will hurt ye. Stand up." She reeled back protesting as he helped her to her feet. "Leuk."

Brenawyn gulped and squeezed her eyes shut, but turned around to face the forest. Her body thrummed with tension, but she gave an audible breath and relaxed a hair. The moment she opened her eyes, he could feel the recognition in his contact with her. She looked at the wolf in the distance. It sat with its head cocked to the side, one ear flopped over, looking as amiable as Spencer, but much bigger. Alex released her arms to allow her greater movement and she swung on him. "The wolf? It's you?"

"Nay, definitely no', but t'is difficult ta explain. Are ye familiar with Plato's theory o' Forms?"

"I'm not sure. Philosophy class was a long time ago."

"He postulated that non-material things—concepts such as justice, love, equality—had an ideal, perfect form that existed elsewhaur. Those concepts in reality would be a copy o' the original form, but no matter how advanced, because they were a copy, would ne'er come close ta being the actual Form. We create these copies, but we canna imagine the true Form, so the concept is destined ta always remain imperfect."

"Ok. So what does that have to do with … "

"Plato was wrong. His premise was based on the wrong sequence o' creation. The actual order is that the universe created the Forms haur, in response ta the creation o' each o' the species. The wolf," he indicated the animal in the distance, "was created from the life force o' e'ery wolf in existence for all time. That wolf is *the* Wolf."

"It is perfect? Everything here is perfect?"

"Aye. Everything besides us."

"When you changed in the kitchen … "

"I am connected ta the wolf. When I changed, ye saw that wolf. I can … how do I explain? I can call the Form ta me. The laws o' physics still hold, two objects canna occupy the same space, so when I call a Form, part o' me, the physical part, comes haur, just as the physical part o' the Wolf goes thaur. The transition is painful. T'is no' common for the body and the consciousness ta be separated."

"So, when you changed your mind was there, in the body of the wolf?"

"Essentially, aye. Though, t'is a little tougher ta keep perspective, because instinctual behavior must no' reside in the mind. So, t'is harder ta keep focused. I doona transform often for that reason."

"Instinctual behavior?"

"Hunting, mating … "

Brenawyn turned away to hide her blush remembering his state when he turned back.

"Brenawyn, t'is also how I kent ye crossed over. Yer grandmother didna ha' ta tell me."

"Oh." Silence stretched out and at some point, the wolf padded over to stand in front of her. She didn't cringe away but stood her ground mesmerized. She reached a tentative hand out, and the wolf cautiously closed the distance. Her fingers brushed the soft pelt and she stepped closer burying both her hands in his soft fur. The animal half closed his eyes in the luxury of the caress but his ears sprang alert and he raised his head, stepping in front of her as a shield.

The underbrush rustled. "Nothing will hurt ye haur, Brenawyn," Alex said behind her as the bear emerged.

The wolf was big, but the bear was enormous. It too held back and sniffed the air for their scent. Only then did it approach. "You have a connection with the bear too?"

"Aye." Again, she held out her hand, and the bear responded. "Though, I hope ye are no' around when I change."

"Why, is that?"

Alex approached. "Look at the bear's fur. The fur is thick, much thicker than the wolf's. Thaur is an outer coat and a much thicker undercoat, harder ta penetrate. The thick coat, combined with the thicker hide, sharp claws and teeth, can kill prey in seconds. If I turn, run. I'll buy ye time."

"Stop. You're scaring me."

"Honestly, that is no' my intention, and I havena touched on the scary parts yet."

"You haven't?"

"Just wait. Ye'll find out soon enough. Thaur is still the leopard and the hawk ye need ta meet."

"Why are you showing them to me?"

"The wolf I use for tracking. The wolf's sharp sense

o' smell canna be compared ta anything else. The bear for attack power, the leopard for stalking, and the hawk, for its keen eyesight. Ye need ta know this because I am yer protector for now, out o' necessity," *and for eternity if ye'll ha' me.*

"I still think you have the wrong girl. I'm nobody."

"Ye willna kin so for long. Come, Oghma awaits."

"Who's Oghma?"

"Ye will find out soon enough, and ye'll meet my mother."

"You mean your mother is a goddess?"

"Aye, Goddess of the Moon."

Brenawyn stopped him with a hand on his arm, "Holy shit! A goddess?" She shook her head.

Alex nodded and continued walking.

As the dense forest gave way to the clearing, Alex's anxiety grew. There would be no turning back afterward. The fallacy of choice would be completely stripped from Brenawyn as she took her place as the rightful heir of the high priestess' office. He should have prepared her for this somehow. To blame Leo Callaghan was senseless; little did her actions years before affect the present. The prophecy had proclaimed this future in its vague, noncommittal way. What will be, will be with prophecy, leaving everything to damned fate. No one had a choice. Everything, everyone, played a part as pawns in a twisted design. No happiness, no fulfillment other than that of the planned destiny played out—but to whose happiness and fulfillment? He was jealous of those who thought they had achieved it. He would not sit by and allow Brenawyn to be used, even if she didn't know why he behaved the way he did. Let that be a mystery. He would not let one more person be a pawn.

Oghma was sitting by the Well of Seagis trailing fingers in the water when they cleared the forest edge. Alex knew that their presence was announced well before they had stepped through the tree line. He took Brenawyn's hand, giving a slight squeeze for reassurance, and led her to the Well. Only then did Oghma look up. His long gray hair was swept back and clubbed, his face devoid of wrinkles, but wisdom and age were reflected in his eyes. His rich dark robes were of heavy brocade with silver embroidery edging the lapels, wide sleeves, and hem; under them he wore pants of plain brown velvet. Though he was sitting, it was easy to determine that his robes were designed to trail after him. Despite the volume and femininity of garb, it did nothing to detract from his small yet masculine stature. The only jewel he wore was one large opal tie tack.

He rose from his seat and bowed slightly. "Ah, you have brought her." His speech was unique. It lacked any accent and dialectical colloquialisms, syllables enunciated with precision, volume, intonation, and timing perfect. It was musical and alluring. Brenawyn mused that he would make the most tedious legal affidavit or recitation of the dictionary sound stimulating. He turned to Brenawyn, and smirking, cocked his head to the side. "Come, you who are lost and blind, come lay your troubles down. It will all be well momentarily."

Oghma turned to Alex dismissing him out of turn.

"You are no longer needed." But before he could flick his wrist in dismissal, Alex spoke up defensively, "I am her protector."

"Do you dare to suggest that she is in danger from me, child?"

"I meant nay disrespect, but I will remain. She has no' the upbringing o' an initiate. She kens nothing o' the Auld Ways."

The golden eyes flared red, a matching red rosacea from broken blood vessels spread in spider webs under the skin over his cheeks. He took a breath and opened his mouth.

"Please, let him stay. I'm so ... he has agreed to be my protector. Please."

Gazing into Brenawyn's eyes, Oghma's ire slowly evaporated, taking the red stain from his cheeks and the pigment from his eyes. As he did, he looked so beautiful, one could weep. He bowed again, "As ye will, but remain there. Keep your distance, protector. I will not have interference." Then turning to Brenawyn, he considered her for a long moment, circling her. "Child, long were the days we have waited for your coming. Tell me. Why have you come now?"

Brenawyn looked back to Alex pleadingly, but her chin was grabbed and forced back to look at Oghma. "Child, the answer you seek lies not with him. Tell me, why now?"

"I   don't ... I   don't ... know.   I ... have   these memories. They're jumbled together, but they're contradictory and disjointed. Alexander said that you can

58

help. Can you? Can you clear my head and tell me what to believe?"

"Wait, Brenawyn ... "

Oghma turned to him eyes blazing, "Silence, Protector." Turning back to Brenawyn, "Your eyes are clouded, I see. I will clear them, but my intervention will not bring answers. Those answers are rooted in the motives of men. I cannot give you what you seek. I can only set you on the path of discovery."

"My memory is blurry; I can't tell if anything is real. I have these old memories of a loving relationship but childless, fused to the new memories of the miscarriage and ... " shaking her head, "abuse, I think. I need to know which to believe. What do you need me to do?"

"The water that bubbles up from the earth here is special, giving the fruit that falls in a power that is not there when it grows on the tree. Go and retrieve one from the bottom. You must be the one to choose."

Brenawyn waded into the water, pleasantly surprised by its warmth. The pool was deeper than it appeared, she would have to sink to retrieve anything from the bottom. With a sharp intake of breath, she submerged, then quickly came back to the surface holding a single nut from the bottom of the pool. Holding it in her closed fist, she swam the short distance to where Oghma sat on the bank. "Stay in the water. It will help ease the pain."

"The pain?"

"Yes, child, did not your protector tell you? The human mind is a complex thing and the magic that affects it intricate, so as to not drive the individual mad." He

59

paused, and looked into her eyes. "Are you mad? You do not seem to be, though it makes little difference." He broke contact, but did not step back. "The spell to remove such an intricate working is not delicate. There is no way for me, as powerful as I am, to know the depth and avenues your mind has taken to this incantation. It will be painful because I will have to rip them from your mind, whereas they were strategically placed before. Are you still willing?"

"Yes."

"Good. This is the Well of Seagis, the well of knowledge. The nut you hold is the key. Eat the nut and your true memories will take hold, expelling the false, forcing them to surface." Oghma turned to Alex. "Boy, make yourself useful."

Alex waded in to kneel behind Brenawyn, "Lean back." Brenawyn looked confused, wary. "By touching, ye'll be able ta use my strength ta help ye better deal with the pain."

"No, I don't want you in pain."

"Sh. I willna be in pain. I'll just be lending some o' my strength ta ye. I'll be fine. Doona worry. Eat the nut."

Brenawyn settled against him, crackled the softened shell in her hand and picked out the pieces. She chewed and swallowed, not surprised when nothing happened. She sat looking at the image of the purple sky reflected in the surface of the water, at the dragonfly buzzing close to the surface, and at the frog on the bank off to the side of her vision. She turned her head to Alexander who sat cradling her body, her hands on his thighs as she sat crossed legged on the silty bottom of the well.

"The fruit that you just willingly ingested is the knowledge of all things. To eat it," said Oghma as he cracked open another water-softened shell, "is to open yourself to that infinite truth. From the beginning of time to its end, knowledge will always be power. In the Old Ones' great intuition, they granted favor in this well, but it does not come easily. For a prize such as this, the effort of will is necessary to seek the truth. You have given your consent when you asked to have the haze lifted from your mind. Once asked, gladly given. Once done, it cannot be undone. You will pass a threshold from which you can never return. Do you understand this, initiate?"

Her body bowed in that moment, racked and rigid with pain, Alex moved to cradle her close to him, and pour his strength into her, but it wasn't enough. He repositioned her and pried her mouth open, and before he thought, his head swooped down to take her open mouth. He was batted away by an unseen force, but it was too late, Brenawyn's pain was now his and his alone. He clawed at his head, fighting vainly to relieve the pressure, vomiting bile and sludge in the clear waters of the Well before sinking in the blessed arms of the warm water and oblivion.

CHAPTER 6

Oghma settled down and purposely eased the tension in his body, waiting for one or another god to arrive. They were impatient; and to rely on such a weak-willed species with the delicacies of staving off another war was near unconscionable. But it was not his to say.

He was surprised that it was Nimue who appeared first.

"Greetings, brother. How dae ye pass the day?"

"Interestingly enough," Oghma indicated the floating forms of priestess and her protector. "I thought that you might find it worthy of remark that your son has chosen to be her protector."

Nimue raised an elegant eyebrow, "Did he now?" She stepped closer to the edge, turning her back to Oghma considering the two. "So chance intertwined the fates o' those famed, ta be rejoined and set right when legacy is reclaimed." She sighed, and then turned to face him. "It doesna surprise me at all. He is his father's son after all; thaur is a sense o' honor in all the Sinclair line." She smiled, gaining a far-off look in her eye, "His father once offered ta champion for me, though he kent thaur was no need."

Oghma bowed, "Just so then."

"What did ye glean from the removal o' the last o' yer bindings?"

"Lines are being drawn and sides taken. As always, some wait to see the outcome. I do not worry over these. Those who claim to be with us are silent, though they are witnesses. Be wary. All who claim allegiance should not be trusted."

"Noted."

"As for the priestess … "

"The would-be priestess, she has no' given her consent fully yet."

"As you say. She is unique. She can defend herself—actually fend off an attack. I smelt the burned flesh before I saw the ruin of what had been his right forearm. She healed her dog. Made a successful attempt at shape-shifting, stripped an Oracle of her ability, and helped in a resurrection spell."

Nimue gasped. "How? She looks so … "

"Feeble? Weak? Mortal?"

"Aye."

"This I do not know, but she did it without preparation, training, or even the rudimentary knowledge of how it worked."

Nimue rounded on him, pressing him to the ground. A stone shard dug painfully into his back. "Are ye telling me that she is anomalous, operating outside the bounds o' fate and prophecy?"

Oghma pushed back against Nimue's weight and sat up. "That is not all."

"Tell me quickly."

"She has an affinity for animals and can make the elements rise to her call."

A sharp intake of breath and all noise of the forest and its life suddenly fell silent. "If it is how ye say, then the prophecy has come full circle, and we are looking at long last inta a possible end o' times. Thaur will be several entities that willna stop until they wrest the power from her hands. Though this time I kin they will try ta kill her before she gives birth ta her progeny. She willna come inta her full power until then."

~ ~ ~

Falling. The edge of the stair rushed up to make painful contact with her temple. She twisted to take the brunt on her side, protecting the baby, but end over end, heart pounding in her ears, she couldn't control the momentum. Arms cradled her bulging stomach. Bruising contact, twice, an echoing crack and pain lanced up her arm, thrice, wrenching as a foot caught in the spindles. To land in a crumpled broken heap facedown, her weight pressing down and an answering stabbing pain before oblivion.

Brenawyn sat up in time to be violently sick in the long grass rushes on the bank. The heaving stopped, but she hung her head there not willing to move else another memory force its way in. Her hair hung in wet clumps, clinging to her face. She didn't care. When she was sure that she wasn't going to vomit again, she sat back on her haunches, wiped the residual spittle from her mouth with the back of her arm, and slicked her wet hair back from her forehead. Oh God, what the hell happened?

Her limbs felt heavy and it took all her concentration to breathe. In, out, in, out.

The pounding headache was gone, the pressure in her chest easing. She knew that she was changed, but how—she didn't want to explore. Yet. Let her get her normal faculties back. Have her arms and legs respond when she wanted to move.

Feeling came back into her fingers and toes first, sharp tingling caused her to stretch the joints to ease the discomfort. The prickling radiated to the lower extremities. Inhaling through her teeth, she gritted against the pain as she flexed her toes, her calves, against the contracting muscles.

Memories came flooding back unbidden and a new nausea bubbled up. She tried to swallow the bile that was knowledge. Knowledge of the truth. Why? Why couldn't she go back to the way it was before? It was easier to mourn Liam, the husband she thought she remembered. Those memories were gone. Did she even remember them? It must have been easier than this, to know without a doubt the man he was. What happened? How did he do this to her? How was he capable?

Sunshine and sweetness replaced by moodiness and

sullenness in turn, losing patience and roaring at nothing, as if someone flipped a switch after we returned from our honeymoon. Shock when he first hit me, a stinging slap to the cheek, leaving a partially swollen eye. I never pleased him. He was always waiting for something, observing, rarely patient.

Once-soft memories of intimate, tender moments shared between husband and wife, replaced by moments of shame and humiliation. Face shoved into the pillow as he pumped into me from behind. Always behind.

Hospitals. A variety of emergency rooms. Never giving anyone a hint. Black eyes, bruised sides, broken bones ... so many broken ribs. The reasons varied, accidents all, or most. There was that time he made me report it as an assault. Of course, not by him.

Then I got pregnant.

He seemed so ... pleased with himself for a time.

He stopped hitting me. Stopped touching me. Stopped looking at me.

All I felt was relief.

Snap.

I didn't even see him. Realization and knowledge hit me at the same time as the boot to my lower back at the top of the stairs.

She glanced around and gasped, Alexander was floating face down. Gaining her feet, she trudged through the knee-deep water, but slipped into the deeper center, she swam to where he lay, "Alex. Alex. Please." She grabbed his shirt and heaved his body over. Buoying his head up against her chest, she hooked an arm under his and backpedaled out of the water. The reed-covered bank was near, but the hard part of dragging his limp body was here too. She scrambled around, clasping him under the arms. Sweat beaded on her forehead and she cried out in frustration, "Damn it. You are not going to die on me."

She stood over him, hands clasped still in his armpits, struggling. Planting her feet in the grass she leaned back to move his body infinitesimally. The muscles in her arms screamed as she bent to get a firmer grip again. How long had he been like this? Was it too late? She pulled until just his feet trailed in the water. The surface of the bank would have to do. Damn, why hadn't she kept current on CPR training? How did it go again? She felt for a pulse in the wrist, nothing, in the neck—nothing. She ripped open his shirt, tearing the tails from the waistband of his jeans. Her ear was on his chest but she couldn't hear anything. She straightened. "God, damn it." To the cacophony of the forest, she screamed, "Shut up."

Chest compressions were next. One, two, three … "Come on, please. Don't die." Nine, ten, eleven.

"Most curious."

Brenawyn craned her neck continuing the chest compressions to find Oghma and a woman, even more beautiful, behind a tree not far off. "Help me. Please. He's … he's … I can't even say it. Please."

Oghma slightly bowed his head and retreated leaving the new woman staring inquisitively.

"Why do you do this thing?" she said, flipping her hand to include her actions.

"I'm trying to save him."

"He canna be saved."

"No, don't say that." Brenawyn positioned his head, pinching his nostrils and blew into his mouth, twice. "Oh, God, please, please."

She had seen Alex come back to life once before. Her grandmother claimed he was immortal. But they weren't in the real world any longer. They were here in Tir-Na-Nog. Fairyland. Did the same rules apply here? Brenawyn couldn't be sure. And this goddess was saying he could not be saved. It couldn't be true. Brenawyn frantically resumed her compressions.

She didn't hear the woman approach, but she was there, putting a hand on her shoulder to pull her away. Brenawyn rounded on her, "Please, do something. I'll do anything."

"Anything, child? Forfeit all ye ken. Take yer rightful place as priestess? Dae what ye can ta restore balance?"

"Yes, anything. Just save him."

"I will need a token from ye ta seal the covenant."

"Take it, whatever you want, it's yours." Her arms were screaming. "Do it."

"In time." A jeweled dagger appeared, "I am called Nimue, goddess of the moon." She took Alex's limp arm, slicing across his palm. The blood barely oozed from the wound and Brenawyn threw herself, ear to his chest, no heartbeat.

"Please, do it now, and I'll give you all you want and more."

But Nimue didn't hasten her movements, she took Brenawyn's wrist, yanked it toward her, and sliced across the palm. Brenawyn didn't feel it, but next thing she knew Nimue was pressing the wounds together. "By yer vow yer fates are intertwined." She grabbed a lock of Brenawyn's hair under her right ear and with a swipe of the blade cut it close to her scalp.

Outraged at the further violation, Brenawyn pulled her head away. "Hey, enough. Save him now."

Nimue ran her fingers down the length of the lock and looped it around her arm, tying in loosely around her armored bicep. "A token o' yer oath. Be glad it wasna more. Now repeat after me."

Brenawyn harrumphed, and pleaded, "Please!"

"Repeat."

"Yes, Yes, anything."

"I gi' my blood oath," Nimue paused when hesitation registered on Brenawyn's face. "Dae ye want me ta save his life?"

"Yes, all right. I give my blood oath."

"Good. Ta protect Alexander Morgan Sinclair, son o' Robert Sinclair, grandson o' Donald Sinclair, claiming him as my own." She looked over at Brenawyn. "Say it."

Brenawyn rushed through the words, "To protect Alexander Sinclair, son of Robert Sinclair, grandson of Donald Sinclair, claiming him as my own."

"His life is more sacred and dear than my own, and if I am ta fail, may I wander endlessly without the eternal reward."

"And, I have your promise that you'll do everything you can to save him?"

"Hurry, girl. His light dwindles as ye hesitate."

Brenawyn tore her eyes away to start chest compressions again as she repeated the last lines.

Nimue batted Brenawyn away and placed her hand on his chest. Scrolls lit up her arm and Alex's red defensive ones responded. His chest rose, pushing her hand up until his back was bowed, arms out akimbo. He groaned, the first sign of life, and Brenawyn let out a breath she hadn't known she was holding, relieved.

Nimue eased him back down, curiously, she brushed a stray lock of hair off his forehead and bent to kiss his forehead. "He canna be saved, but he still lives. He exists for the pleasure o' the Hunter."

"I don't understand."

A smile played on her lips, "Alexander Morgan Sinclair is the favored quarry o' the Wild Hunt. He will be pursued throughout time because he has shown himself ta be … interesting."

Brenawyn put her hand on his chest to assure herself that he, in fact, lived. He was hot. Too hot? The question ran through her mind. His chest rose and fell in shallow yet even breaths. Hesitant to break the connection, she turned to look over her shoulder, "The Wild Hunt? What is the Wild Hunt?"

"Why is it that ye ken nothing? Ha' ye no' learned? Who was yer teacher? This lack o' education canna be abided."

"Teachers? There were many throughout the years but somehow I don't think this is what you are referring to. In what way is my education lacking?"

"Ye are unfamiliar with yer gods."

"No. I am familiar, quite familiar, with my God."

"Doona anger me, child. Doona assume anything from my meager appearance. I appear this way because t'is the only way yer puny mind can process my existence." Nimue looked at her reflection in the water and held her hands out. Almost absentmindedly, she traced the lines of the palm of her hand, and scowled in disgust. "It is insufficient." Getting to her feet, she strode away, then twisted back to face Brenawyn, "I am magnificent, blindingly beautiful in my power. All the gods are uniquely so, but ye humans and yer delicate minds. So many went mad with the revelation. Ye are useless, yer race, in so many ways. So flawed. Living the life o' a single flame, consuming all around ye, until the very end as if ye ken it was yer last, ye glow brighter for a few infinitesimal moments and then, ye are dust again. Ye struggle so against the inevitable, but t'is ... most interesting."

"I ... I don't understand."

"T'is no' for ye ta kin the ponderings o' a god. Come, I will serve as yer teacher in this."

"No, what happens if he needs me. I have to stay here."

"Suit yerself then."

With a sudden sensation of freefalling, Brenawyn found herself on the mossy ground in the familiar copse of trees staring up at the night sky through the branches with her heart ready to explode in her chest. She gasped for air. Disoriented from the connection loss, she sat and saw her grandmother's house in the distance. She crawled to Alex

71

when he started to stir. She did what she could in her weakened condition to turn him on his side, helping him to vomit out ingested water and bile. Odd, to be vomiting water as one almost drowned, because he was completely dry. He collapsed again, but his chest rose and fell with regularity and his pulse was steady.

"Be calm, he stirs. Are ye ready for the lesson ta begin?"

Brenawyn jumped and swung to face Nimue, who had obviously followed them through. "If you are omnipotent, why are you being so magnanimous? A mere human—who insulted your very existence?"

Her eyes glowed iridescent and her jaw tightened. "It has been agreed, though it pleases me no'. Even with extended life as the high priestess, yer life will be over before the leaves on the Tree o' Knowledge in Tir-Na-Nog fall for the season. All beings are chained by fate. Yer fate has been written, but it is no' the only possibility. The covenant," brushing the ends of her lock of hair, "makes it a stronger prospect, but we must no' falter in our aims for the alternative is unacceptable.

"Once was a time that we were strong, a time before the Great War that had us retreat ta Tir-Na-Nog. This was the beginning o' our downfall, helped by yer ancestor. We found it curious, her struggle to save the child. She was unwise ta do so, many were angered by her abuse o' her meager talents. A great argument resulted. Some called for her death, ta be sacrificed as old—some still do. Calling on powers only a god possesses! The insolence! Ta attempt the Phoenix, an incantation reserved for the perpetuation o' beliefs. And perhaps if it was just her action, her blasphemy, she would ha' been compelled ta sacrifice herself if not for the other factor.

"Which was?"

"Brighit was Cernunnos' lover. She was burned a' the stake for her beliefs by those that professed belief in yer merciful deity. Before she died, she offered her child ta the universe. The Phoenix again, but only half—the other half. Again, cast for love."

"So, it comes down to a matter of supply and demand?"

"Hmm?"

"Supply and demand. According to the story, the soul is released and because my grandmother called out for what? Help? Whatever. It's not as if I believe this, but for argument's sake, she lit the overhead register light? Called AAA? Called for your help, essentially, and it was granted? Why?"

"As I said before, we ken it was love that motivated her, just as it was for Brighit, which we found out too late, but that's whaur yer protector comes in."

"Love? So what?"

"Doona be so flippant. The concept is interesting. What one o' ye will dae for this so-called love. It interested us and thaurfore we granted the fusion o' soul and body in utero. The result—ye. Or so he believes. Though, for argument's sake, he has thought so several times 'afore throughout these six hundred years.

"Alexander is six hundred years old?"

"In the eternal servitude o' the Wild Hunt and

thaurfore by extension, the Hunter, Cernunnos, yes, ta yer mind, he is just over six hundred years old, but within that time, has died dozens o' times, subject ta the Hunt."

"What? Wait, slow down … I'm getting confused."

"I see this will take more time. Perhaps, I shall put the memories o' these events in yer mind and be done with the ordeal o' having ta explain in small words."

"No," she said, backing away from the goddess. "You will do no such thing. Stay out of my head, lady. God or no, stay out."

"Child, ye doona yet kin, I can dae anything I please ta ye, Alexander, Leoncha, Maggie, or yer dog quivering on the door o' yer abode. But for the sake o' the agreement, I will try ta curb my impatience and let ye 'process the new information' as I believe he worded it."

"Who worded it?"

"Alexander bargained for ye."

"All right, we'll come back to that. Tell me about the Wild Hunt. How is Alex involved?

"As long as thaur was memory, memory o' the gods, we ha' existed. No beginning and no end. But before this, the concept o' fate existed solely. This is why the gods are subject ta fate as well. T'is the way o' the universe. The universe requires balance, good paired with evil, light paired with dark. Polar opposites. This is one o' the tenants o' the universe's make up. The Wild Hunt exists, in part, ta meet the demand o' balance. Hunter paired with the hunted."

"So bad versus good?"

"Is a lion evil when it tracks and brings down the

gazelle? No. T'is just in both creatures' nature ta be that which they are. So the Hunt is merely that, pursuit and capture on the field."

"How did Alex become involved, because I gather you have been around for more than six hundred years?"

"Cernunnos was enraged at Brighit."

"And he had her punished before he had time to realize she did what she did to save the child," Brenawyn surmised.

"Aye, he seethed and ranted, and the underworld shook. He only saw the sacrilege, what he thought was sacrilege."

"He thought she was aborting the pregnancy."

"Hmm … aye, in a way. He thought she was discarding the honor o' bearing a god's child. By the time he figured it out, it was too late. The child's soul was lost ta time and Brighit was insane, driven thaur by Cernunnos."

Brenawyn walked to the edge of the clearing, keeping her back turned Nimue. It was against her instincts, but she needed time to process. The story Alex had told her in the car a few days ago, could it be true? In any other time, place, instance, she would chalk the whole thing up to wild imaginations. Hell, she had a vivid one herself, but too many unexplainable things had been happening of late. "Cernunnos found Alex, didn't he?"

Brenawyn turned to find Nimue looking down at the prostrate form of Alex, "Alexander was raised ta be the next Shaman o' the Order, the voluntary recipient o' the memory o' perpetual belief. He underwent the Rite o' the

Phoenix at the age o' thirty. As Shaman, much like the priestess, his life is extended far beyond … ten times the span o' a single human's life or more, a perfect candidate for the search for the child.

At first, this seemed ta placate Cernunnos, but as yer centuries passed and no sign of the lost one, Cernunnos became unreasonable. It was interchangeably our fault, Brighit, humans and their fear o' what they doona ken, and finally Alexander. After the third failed attempt at finding her, Cernunnos tore Alex's soul from his body, the first declaration o' new quarry, and the Hunt began. Even with his extended years as Druid Shaman, he was a mere mortal so the first Hunt ended shortly after it had begun. With the first resurrection, the first o' many to transform him inta something else, he had heightened ability—a result of the completion o' the Hunt ta be more o' a challenge next time.

"How many times?"

"Often enough, but no' consistently, though now that ye ha' been found, perhaps Cernunnos will lose interest in him. Each time he has been brought back it was with additional abilities. Alexander is the most powerful Shaman that will ever live and yet he is chained at the neck unable ta help himself for all eternity despite his heightened abilities."

"Can't Cernunnos release him?"

"No. Once quarry, quarry he will remain, e'er ta be tied ta the hunting grounds. Even a god canna break the bond. Alexander is now part o' the eternal quest for balance."

"What of his soul?"

"Once Cernunnos held that, though now it is beyond even him … destroyed by the machinations of devious minds. Doona be concerned for his soul. His destiny didna turn out as he hoped, but he kent the cost o' the commitment. To say he would protect ye with his life doesna apply ta this situation, because in death he will come back stronger. He is devoted and relentless. He will protect ye until yer powers exceed his own."

"So my vow was unnecessary?"

Brenawyn saw the answer reflected in the goddess slight smile and glowing eyes. A wave flew from her fingertips and hit Alex as he lay on the ground, immediately waking him. He slowly gained his feet, but when he did Brenawyn could see it wasn't under his own power. His head hung between his shoulders and his body slumped as if an invisible force were holding him up.

"Hey, what are you … "

"An example ta allay yer fears. Leuk and learn." She turned her attention to Alex, "Leuk alive, Shaman, and show her what ye are." His head snapped up and murder was emblazoned on his face.

Jaw set, "A'richt, Mother."

"Mother?"

Alex sneered and nodded his head in disgust. "The dog and pony show is tired and how many times do I ha' ta tell ye that I am no' yers ta put on display."

Nimue surged at him forcing his chin down with a strength that belied her frame, "And when will ye learn, my *bright* boy that I doona care what ye kin. Ye will do as

77

ye are told." She held her fingers up over her head, and tore at the air. Nothing happened at first, but then a slight distortion in the air beyond the deity's hand began to grow. Brenawyn rubbed at her eyes, but Alex's response was all she needed. His eyes grew wide and he would have cowered away if not for the vice on his chin. Brenawyn was not hallucinating. "Or would ye prefer ta catch the attention o' the Hunter again? The transformations are getting harder ta bear, are they no'? Without me, ye'd be crawling, begging for yer life ta end. Nothing would be real but the pain."

Pleading, "No, please. I humbly apologize. Doona drop the glamour. Please, no' yet. I canna go back yet."

Nimue considered him for a moment and must have been satisfied because with a flick of her wrist the distortion was gone, she patted his cheek and she released him. "Be a good boy and show her."

Brenawyn, stepping forward stammered, "Please, he … he doesn't need to show me anything. I've seen him turn into a wolf. I don't have any doubts about his strength. Please. You're his mother. How could you do this to him?"

She swiveled to face Brenawyn, "I am losing my patience at yer insolence, child. Doona make the mistake ta cross me again. Agreement or no'." Looking back at Alex she said, "prophecy or no', nothing will remain of ye but ashes."

"Brenawyn, *a chuisle mo chroi,* understand that she means every word. Step back and be forewarned. The wolf was," ripping his shirt over his head, she heard the familiar cracking of bones, "just the beginning." The rending of denim came next as his body, wracked with pain, crouched. Brown fur sprouted and ran along his back like a chain of dominos, creaking as muscle massed under the new pelt. Grunts gave way to the growl of the bear she saw in the other realm. The same? Was it the same? Just as the transformation was complete, the Bear—Alex—bent again, the cracking of bone rang out sickening loud against the wall of the forest around them. Riveted, she watched as the thick brown pelt was replaced by the spotted hide of a leopard. Standing in place, where just seconds before stood the bear, now a leopard stared at Brenawyn. Without breaking the gaze, the leopard hunched down, lower than the bear. Popping and cracking, the leopard cried out, panted, a second cry cut short by the lonely shriek of a hawk. Feathers replaced the spotted fur, lastly developing on arms turned wings. This was the same hawk, just as it was the leopard, the bear, and the wolf. Brenawyn stood horrified and Alex beat his wings. Small whirlwinds loosed dirt and pebbles as he took flight.

Brenawyn ducked, not out of necessity, but rather reflex. She watched as he flapped his wings to get above the tree line and then glide in wide lazy circles once, twice, three times before coming down to land in the same spot. The hawk stood with his wings out and the change came again. Molting feathers, which disappeared before hitting the ground, left the dusky skin of Alex standing naked in all his glory. His manhood jutted out from his body and Brenawyn felt her cheeks flame and she looked away, glancing at Nimue, who stood off to the side looking, surprisingly, at her.

Nonplussed at the events or his state of arousal, Brenawyn had no time to consider the machinations of this crazy bitch and looked at Alex again. His runes glowed red and blue starting on his chest and racing outward—torso, abdomen, legs; he was covered. She gasped in horror as out of the corner of her eye she saw a man of sorts, made of mud and rock, rush at Alex. He held a blade of deepest black and Alex met him unarmed. The assailant swung wide, but Alex pivoted and feinted, over and over, moving the fight closer to the tree line. Brenawyn followed at a distance, looking for anything she could use as a weapon. If his mother could sit idly back and do nothing, wait … she sent the damn thing. *Shit, I have to do something.* But what? A gun would be good. A sword, though she had doubts that she'd be able to lift it to bring it down with any force. Force enough to what? Distract it for a moment and hopefully Alex could do whatever he was going to do? Time enough for him to get whatever weapon he was going to get. What the hell was she thinking? Shit. *Think, Brenawyn. Think. What the fuck is happening! Now would be a good time to wake up.*

But she knew that she was awake. Alex gained the oak and planted his feet wide, back braced against the trunk. In seconds that seemed like years, she saw the dark blade come down on Alex's exposed neck. She screamed.

The man jumped. Odd. And stopped for the fraction of a second, enough for Alex to grab the blade of the sword. Alex's runes grew brighter as he yanked the sword from the man's grip. Blood dripped from his own hand, but he was able to grip the pommel with both hands.

Forcing the creature back, Alex hacked at his exposed parts: an arm, an outstretched leg. Shearing off bits of what looked like … mud. How could that be?

Alex advanced and brought the battle perilously close to where she stood. Brenawyn gasped as Alex threw the sword, skewering his opponent through the head, but yet the creature fought on, swinging mechanically. Alex, apparently having enough of the fight, stepped into the opponent's swing. He put his hand on the chest of the thing, ripped out the blade and said a few words that Brenawyn couldn't understand. The thing's chest exploded scattering mud in a wide circle. Brenawyn ran to his side sliding on her knees the last few feet just as Alex hit the ground. "What the hell was that?"

"A construct. Nimue favors them. T'is nothing more than a small portion o' will poured inta a bit o' indigenous earth. A parlor trick, anyone with a shadow o' talent can do them. The number that they can control is what separates the men from boys, or in this case, deities from mortals. I kin ye willna believe it, but she was being kind. This was a demonstration o' my abilities and t'is no' over. Before t'is done ye'll see the monster I am."

Brenawyn moved closer, but the brush of his leg against hers brought the reality of what he had named himself to the front of her mind. She stumbled back, trying to focus her eyes on anything but … "Are you all right?"

Alex wiped at his forehead. "I'm fine. Am pure done in. Quick transformations are draining. In the field, such a display is never used. Wastes precious seconds, and seconds can win or lose a battle."

The hairs on the back of Brenawyn's neck tingled and she knew without looking that Nimue was there. "Let us continue the demonstration."

"Enough, Mother. She's seen enough for today. I hold ye ta our agreement."

Her head cocked to the side, and with what could be seen as motherly love, for those that had the fortune not to see the origins of the struggle, she glided over, for Brenawyn did not see her feet move, to caress Alex's cheek. "Ta our agreement," she said, turning to bow to Brenawyn, "and ta the covenant. Rest now, son. Take yer ease with the mother o' yer child if ye choose. The time is quickly approaching."

CHAPTER 7

Fireflies glinted here and there, even though it was too late in the evening for them. They floated in, multiplying until they were a veil of twinkling lights around Nimue lifting wisps of her hair, the edges of her clothes, and then the space she occupied was empty. She was gone, the fireflies with her. The surrounding forest let out a sigh and Brenawyn could hear the sounds of the forest again, creatures flitting in the trees, scurrying under the brush. Spencer whined on the edge of the clearing, Leo or Maggie must have let him out, and he had found her. He sniffed the air and crept over, tentatively at first, but once past an invisible barrier he ran and hit Brenawyn mid-chest, and managed to wiggle, lick her face, and stand over her defensively in unison. "It's all right, boy. I'm fine."

She scuttled over to Alex, scooting the last few feet on her rear. He sat with his leg outstretched, staring intently at the back of the house in the distance. He jumped when she touched him, going for the sword automatically. "Whoa, easy, it's just me."

He sighed and reached for her hand, "Och, aye, t'is you. Are ye well, lass?"

Brenawyn laughed stiffly, "Are you?"

"Aye, I am sound. I meant," he touched her temple, "haur, lass. Are ye a'richt?"

"I got what I asked for, stuff for new nightmares. God, I was so stupid. What was real? Was it always abusive, did he shows signs early on? Putting that aside, because Lord knows, I'll never be able to get a handle on that. How he treated me. Why did I put up with it? Why didn't anyone tell me?"

"Ye should ken why, Brenawyn."

"Oghma said that he can't give me insight into men's motives."

"Ye already ha' it. Ye lived with the man for years 'afore his death, and e'en if the memory binding was in place, thaur were hints. What dae ye ken? This behavior, these actions, and the medallion ye found hidden in his belongings—he was a practitioner, wanting ta access yer latent abilities. The memory bindings were in place for years, three a' the very least, since his death, and possibly from the verra beginning, or a' least from the time he had access ta yer grandmother's attic for the first o' the three placements, the third was probably the one ye found first. He wouldna ha' thought that he was going ta die, and barring that ye wouldna go through his belongings.

Knowing Oghma the way I dae, for the phrasing of

yer request, 'tell me what ta believe' thaur has ta be more. What did he reveal ta ye?"

"I can't even think straight, and you want me to recall a detailed conversation? Wait, before I get into that, how about, what the fuck just happened?

I can almost … almost make sense of Oghma—I can't believe I'm saying that. I mean, it's like I just went to fairyland and met a god and a goddess, and I'm okay with that." Brenawyn paused. "Holy shit. I think I'm okay with that! Jesus Christ, I need to be committed." She heard her voice increase an octave, and felt the hysterics bubble up, "I mean I'm ready for the 'nice young men in their clean white coats coming to take me away! HoHo HeHe HaHa. To the funny farm where life is beautiful all the time." she recited from an old song by Jerry Samuels.

Alex's eyebrows shot up. "Calm down. Calm down!" he had Brenawyn by the shoulders at this point, shaking her, "Get yerself together, woman! T'is nay time for being daft."

"Being daft? You want to know who's daft. Your wack-job of a mother! Who does that? Causes their child pain? Puts him in danger?"

Alex burst out laughing. Whatever Brenawyn had expected this wasn't it, which caused him to laugh all the more. "Aye, well, that's what I get for having a, what was the term ye used? A wack-job goddess as a mother."

His reaction sobered her enough to stop her rant. She sat quiet with her hands buried in Spencer's fur as he lay next to her.

After a bit, she turned to him, "I'm sorry. With

85

everything that I have witnessed in the last weeks, I should be more acclimated to," she waved her hand in the air.

Alex nodded in understanding, "I'm sairy lass for the bluntness o' yer exposure; I should ha' found a better way o' preparing ye for yer interview with a goddess. Wording o' requests need ta be carefully constructed but if no' for yer fumbled attempt, ye would still be partially in the dark. Something that we canna ha' for yer own safety."

"Let me see to your wounds. There's a first aid kit in the house. Do you need my help getting up, Alex?"

"No, lass I'm fine." Grunting as he got up, "I doona need the first aid kit, though ye do need the practice at attending wounds. Come, ye'll have yer first lesson as a field medic with me as yer guinea pig." He shuffled off in the opposite direction from the house, holding his side.

"Where are you going?"

"Ah, I'll need more privacy ta shift. T'is mostly exhaustion from shifting, but I think the construct bruised my ribs, perhaps fractured a couple; it hurts ta breathe. If that's true, it will be more painful and I doona want ta attract more attention from the neighbors no matter how far off they are.

Brenawyn followed, unsure of what he wanted her to do. Despite his limping gait, and labored breathing, Brenawyn had to almost jog to keep up. "You're in pain. How can I help?"

"Start back ta the house. I'll be following above."

"Why not spare yourself the pain and walk back with me?"

"Trews, woman, trews. Ye canna expect me ta walk

up ta the house in my altogether."

Brenawyn couldn't help but smile, "You walking out of the trees *in yer altogether,*" affecting a semblance of his accent, "would certainly attract attention."

"Aye, but before we go, lass, thaur needs ta be something settled between us. What were the terms o' yer covenant with Nimue?"

"I don't want to talk about it. Can't we just … "

Alex turned his head away and said, "No. I need ta hear ye say it," barely audible.

Brenawyn wiped her clammy hands on the back of her shorts, "I bargained for your … um, life."

"Damn, ye woman!" Alex paced off, and struck the trunk of the nearest tree with his fist. Leaves rained down on his head, but it was satisfying, so he hit it a few more times, bloodying his knuckles until a premature crab apple clocked him on the top of the head. This gave him pause, and he looked up considering. "I doona ken, why." He looked at the trunk again and splayed his open hand covering an old wound where the tree had lost a mature branch. He hadn't turned to her. "Ye ha' had a hand in raising me from the deid."

Brenawyn approached and reached out to touch his shoulder. "I don't pretend to know how it works, but I'll not regret it. I don't regret it."

He pivoted, and advanced on her. "Perhaps ye doona ken then, or are ye truly daft? I am nay longer a man, for a ha' nay soul. I am an empty husk," indicating his body, "and halfway ta being a shade. I ha' nothing ta offer … I ha' nothing ta offer ye.

"I saw you change and fight. What more is there that I have not witnessed?"

"Magic, beyond shape-shifting, I can call the elements as aids in offensive and defensive magic, simultaneously if necessary, and it usually is."

She crowded him, her ire up, "Well, beast master, magic man, I foreswore my familial connections and my life as I know it and took the mantle of high priestess, all to save you. Our fates are now intertwined."

"No! Say ye didna!" He grabbed her arms pulling her close. "Woman, listen ta me. What were the words ye recited?"

"Um, I, I don't remember exactly."

"Tell me."

"She made me repeat your full name, and the names of your father and grandfather."

"Aye, and what more?"

Brenawyn shook her head, staring off to the side, "Claiming you as my own? And … "

Alex groaned and pushed her to an arm's distance to look in her eyes. "Please lass, say it no' be so. Say ye did not repeat that ye'd wander eternally if ye'd fail a' yer task?"

Tears welled in her eyes. "Well … um." Brenawyn paused to look down for a moment, but almost as quickly as if she decided something, she raised her head locking eyes and whispered, "And if I did?"

Alex pulled her close clutching at her back, trembling. She tilted her face to him, and he claimed her mouth. She pressed her body against him. Hard, he wanted nothing more than to push inside of her, and find his release, his home; filling her with his seed when she quickened around him, but sobering reality struck. Brenawyn was feeling the pull of the blood vow, the instinctual need to consummate.

"Ye doona know what ye ha' done."

"Shush, you talk too much." Brenawyn gripped his shaft, and he groaned, but he put a steadying hand on hers.

"Thaur was a chance for ye 'afore."

Brenawyn pried his hand off of hers and renewed her efforts to stroke him. "I can think of several things you can do with your mouth, and none of them involve speaking."

"Brenawyn, wait, I offered ye a chance ta choose."

"Yes, and I've chosen." She reached behind her back and with one hand unclasped her bra. In one motion, she took both her tee-shirt and undergarment off over her head, and sank to her knees. Her mouth closed on his head, and she moved to take more of him in.

Alex moaned, and she slowed.

"Aye, t'is all for naught. Ye are a slave as much as I am." He put his hands in her hair, and he could feel the vibrations from her amusement, a most intriguing feeling. She splayed her hand on his abdomen, and slowly withdrew scraping her teeth along his shaft. Alex inhaled through his teeth. "Och, woman, that feels good."

After a few minutes of exquisite torture, he could feel the sensation rushing towards its inevitable end. He stepped away before she took him deep again. He raised her so she was standing, and cupped her breasts, his head dipped to suckle and she arched against his forearm braced against her lower back. His free hand found the waistband of her shorts and made quick work of loosening the garment.

His hand slipped inside fingers questing for her hot slick core. She shivered when he rubbed against her sensitivity.

"Please."

"Please what, Brenawyn?"

"Fuck me," she pleaded breathlessly.

Alex chuckled, "in time." He removed his hand, and kissed her opened mouth. "Come."

She laughed, "That's where I was headed before you took your fingers away."

He bit her lower lip and grabbed her ass, bringing her up hard against him, "Aye, I ken that, but ye'll no' thank me for splinters in yer arse later because I ha' a mind ta take ye up against yonder tree."

"I wouldn't mind."

"Just a few steps more we'll be in the shadows completely and thaur's a lovely patch o' moss that I want ta stretch ye out on."

The moss wasn't hard to find and Alex laid her on it bending down to pay homage to one breast then the other. He trailed kisses from the hollow between her breasts, to her rib cage, and her abdomen, before coming to rest at her core, his arms hooked under her legs, hands pressed into her hips. She gasped at first contact of his tongue and rose to meet him making deep guttural sounds of eminent satisfaction. "Woman, I like the sounds ye make," and bent to his task.

A few minutes more brought her to orgasm, and he

moved to rise above her. He pushed himself slowly inside her relishing the tight fit. She reached for him, rocking her hips slightly, and hooked her legs over his. Braced on his forearms, she rose to meet him. Panting in his ear, he turned to take her mouth in breathless kisses. He surged above her and drove his hand under her, his fingers bent to change the angle of her hips. Her panting grew more intense, and she arched against him, finding a rhythm of her own; he matched it feeling the beginning of her climax, he could now seek his own release.

With Brenawyn's head pillowed on his chest, Alex felt satisfied, content, but in the next instant the breeze blew raising goose flesh on her arms. She shivered and sat up, hunting for her discarded clothes. The moment was broken and they'd have to face the new reality her decision created.

Alex returned the smile she gave, and allowed her a few minutes to get dressed. He needed the time too, to put his thoughts into order. She was different, her demeanor screamed it. She was comfortable with him. She sought out his look, his touch. He was able to give this, would always be able to give this; but she deserved more. What would happen when she expected more? He wasn't able to give anymore of himself than this. He wasn't his own man. He was a tool of the gods. He was a product of their might, their muscle ... their monster, a being to do their bidding. It fit their ends for Alex to impregnate Brenawyn. By the gods, he had already done just that. A father. He was going to be a father! For the fraction of a moment, he was gladdened, but reality struck and disgusted with himself, he threw the thought away. She'd have his child true, but he'd never be allowed to be a father to him, he might not even be allowed to see him.

What would that do to her? If she actually had feelings of love for him, and it was too soon to hope for that anyway, the binding would ensure a lifetime of heartbreak, pining for one she could not have. If her motivation was just altruism, it was more heart wrenching. Her binding would drive her mad. She'd be prone to bursts of jealousy and obsession until finally turning violent before turning into a *Dearg Due*, a succubus.

He had bound himself to her too, but he understood the consequences. He knew what was in store. He'd survive, but Brenawyn? It broke his heart that he'd be the source of her pain, and quite probably her undoing.

"Come sit with me 'afore we go back, lass."

Brenawyn came over to sit cross-legged opposite him on the grass.

"Why would ye do it?"

"Do what? Have sex with you?" She looked horrified. "Oh God, didn't you enjoy it?"

"Aye, lass, I did. Verra much so. Nay, that's no' what I meant."

"Then what?"

"The recited words that Nimue … "

"Oh. I shouldn't think it so difficult to figure out. Let's see, my mother, my father, and even Liam, the bastard—all dead. I just couldn't … I couldn't see anyone else...I'm sorry."

"I'm sairy for yer loss, ye know this, but I need ta

think. Yer rash decision sped up the timetable. Normally, a high priestess would take the initiation on Lughnasadh, but ha' a period o' time, three moons, before she had ta claim her right at Samhain. During this time she would train intensively, meditating, communing with nature and that sort o' thing. But ye ha' sworn under a blood oath; that *is* the reason for the new wound across yer palm, that ye succeeded ta the position without the requisite training. Yer more vulnerable than before." *The other reason, he'd omit.*

"What direction is the danger coming from?"

"From the time it was found that yer soul underwent the Phoenix, the Order, a group formed and designated ta keep the balance. Not one member or even the group, in its entirety, could match the potential power o' the priestess but they could stave off the encroaching chaos. Over the centuries, however, a small group splintered from the original, wanting the power for themselves. No' even I, ken the extent o' its membership. The Coven, which they began calling themselves, is only a myth ta some, even some o' the most elder members of our Druid sect. The most immediate threat is Cormac Domhnall MacBrehon and the Oracle he has with him.

"The Oracle, the most dangerous o' the two, is a Vate, an augur, a seer most powerful, but usually in the background. I ha' ne'er heard o' an Oracle traveling out o' the old country. But this one has. 'Afore ye took her abilities back in Salem, she could hypnotize, paralyze, rip ye out o' time and then eviscerate ye like she did ta Barbara, ta me, and all the other sacrifices she has made throughout the centuries ta find you. Believe me, she would too, if she figured out a way ta get her powers back because that is the only way ta wrest yer promising abilities from ye. She is the most dangerous because I wasna immune from her abilities. Even though t'was Cormac who cut me, she ha' done the same ta me and made ye watch too."

"This Cormac is?"

"He's more o' an annoyance with a Napoleon complex. He is as old as myself and was a possible candidate for my clerical position, but the fates chose me and he's never let it go. I can handle him."

"What do you propose we do?"

"Brenawyn, now that ye've made this decision, I ha' ta take ye ta the only place with relative safety. I ha' ta take ye ta my family's castle in Scotland."

"Wait, didn't you tell me that it is nothing but ruins?"

"It appears that way. It must forever remain so, in order ta assure the protection that it offers. But, that is no' exactly *when* I am taking you."

"When? What do you *mean when?*"

"Ye promised ta take yer place as the priestess ta restore the balance. In order ta dae that, ye must dae it from the time the problem arose."

"Do you mean to tell me that when I say goodbye to my grandmother I will nev … never see her again? Never be able to pick up a phone, or open a birthday card?"

"This was why I needed ye ta choose this path only after knowing everything that ye would be giving up. Leo asked me ta go slow with ye in deference ta yer upbringing. She thought it would be too much o' a strain on yer facilities ta ask ye ta believe in a faith so far from yer own. I agreed readily, because I kin what it means ta no' ha' a choice, but now, t'is too late for that. T'will be forced on ye. Unfair, but t'is imperative so I can keep ye and the bairn alive."

"The barn? Bairn … Bairn … You mean baby. Whose baby?

"Our baby."

Brenawyn looked at him with her mouth hanging open, and burst out laughing.

Alex just stared at her. When she sobered, she shook her head. "I'm sorry, Alex. You are mistaken. I'm not pregnant. I can't have children anymore." Brenawyn's face grew hard, and she looked away not bothering to wipe the tears away. "A complication from the miscarriage. Too much scarring."

"I can understand yer resistance ta believe, but time will tell.

CHAPTER 8

Alex still had the problem of approaching the house in his altogether, but it was easily rectified having an example of a domesticated animal so close. It wouldn't cause any comment or raise an alarm seeing a dog emerge from the trees with Brenawyn. For the casual observer, it would just be a woman walking her dog. He put his hand on Spencer's back and felt the shifting of bone and muscle. Spencer turned inquisitively and sniffed at his changing form, but soon abandoned the pair and set off for the house. Alex's ribs were fractured, a painful mending causing him to whimper but new cells replicated and knit the damaged bones. It was not often he shifted into an animal other than the usual four. He was taken aback by the huge similarities of the domesticated dog to that of the wolf. Thousands of years of breeding still had not taken out the pull of instinct. The familiar smells assailed his senses, olfactory sensitivity not in any way diminished.

Brenawyn waited for him at the edge of the clearing and she was silent as they approached the house. He could tell there was something amiss from the moment he stepped foot on the deck. It was too quiet. Where was the dog? Spencer panted like a freight train. He caught his scent locked in a bedroom, silenced but still alive.

She had already flung the screen door open and walked through, not looking back at him. He followed, his animal senses reaching out. He stopped short to avoid bumping into her. She stood a few feet into the kitchen looking at the table.

Leo and Maggie sat facing each other, hands folded identically in front of them, eyes cast down.

"What's going on?"

Leo turned to them, her sigils flaring to life, "Brenawyn!" looking over her shoulder to find a strange dog, "we're not alone."

Alex started to shift, his coat turning a sleek jet black, tail lengthening. He stepped in front, shielding her from the unseen threat. Alex as the leopard hissed and pounced, swatting at the empty air. His attempt was thwarted because of the small space. He did not want to have Leo or Maggie as causalities. The best he could do was try to get Cormac to back up into the living room where there was more space.

"Nana, where's Spencer?"

"Whaur indeed, priestess. Alex, ye need ta change back ta a man 'afore something goes amiss." Cormac appeared in the opposite doorway, hands braced above his head on the lintel. His face was badly swollen on the right side, dark with bruising. He had abrasions on his temple and jawline. "Leuk a' yer handiwork." indicating his face. "T'was just a day ago that I could see out my eye."

The leopard took another swat at him, but Cormac dodged and he quickly grabbed a handful of Maggie's hair yanking her out of her chair. "De ye see what ye did ta me?" She struggled, screaming out. "Ye did quite a job on my bollocks too, but luckily," he forced her hand to his crotch, "I am still whole."

Alex shifted back to human form.

Maggie grunted at his hold, but blurted out through clenched teeth, "I should have killed you, you fucking bastard!"

"Aye, ye tried, nay?" Cormac laughed, "Ye would ha' too, if ye put more o' yer back inta it."

Alex stood, hands covering himself for modesty's sake. "That's enough, Cormac. Yer fight isna with the lass. Let her go."

"Och, Alexander, thaur ye are. I will be taking the priestess off yer hands. Gi' o'er.

"Nay, brother. That I willna dae."

"Your brother?" Brenawyn asked incredulously.

Alex shook his head, "Nay, no' by blood. T'is that we were brothers in cause. We were both members o' the Order, until he became apostate and formed the Coven."

Leo gasped and backed away, "He said as much, but I didn't want to believe him."

"Leo, we have little time. What else did he tell ye?"

"Nothing, um … nothing. It was all … it was all, I

didn't believe him … at all." But she couldn't look Alex in the eye. She turned her back to him.

Alex reached out and touched her shoulder, "Leo, tell me. I can explain. Listen. Stay back, all o' ye. I doona want ye ta get hurt."

Cormac chuckled, "A little late for that now, isn't it, Shaman? Tell us, when did yer faith slip? When did ye start wanting more power? Hmm? Weren't yer abilities enough?

"Leo, Brenawyn, ye ha' ta believe me. Ye ha' this all wrong. I doona want her power, the high priestess' power. I doona want my own—what my own has become. What would I do with it? Trapped as I am in the Wild Hunt.

"As I suspected. Ye are the traitor." Cormac removed his grip in Maggie's hair and forced her down with both hands into the kitchen chair closest to him. "The decision ne'er sat well with me when it was decreed ye be the Shaman, but I ne'er thought for a moment that ye would turn away from our beliefs, so single-minded ye were."

"My convictions ne'er wavered. T'is ye who let yerself be corrupted," Alex replied.

"My friend."

"Doona call me that. Ye ceased ta be that long before the decision was made." Alex approached.

Cormac smiled, put his hands in his pants pockets, and paced away into the living room careful to keep the same distance between them. "Aye, ye are correct o' course. So blinded with rage with the betrayal o' Jamie and Colleen, ye couldn't see the real motivation."

"What are ye blathering about?"

"I manipulated them."

"What?"

"They were fucking each other behind yer back, ye poor bastard, but t'was all she was guilty o' a' that point. I found out well 'afore ye did, felt bad but for a moment, I did. Not a fond memory, finding out first hand that she was cuckolding ye," he laughed, "though she certainly seemed ta be enjoying the attentions o' Jamie as he … "

Alex felt the heat rise, "Damn ye!" Before the decision registered in his mind, he flew at Cormac who sidestepped the blow and sifted time to appear across the room again.

"It went on for months with ye none the wiser. It was shortly after ye had undergone the Phoenix and were *selected* by Cernunnos that the plan came ta me."

"What ha' ye ta do with what happened?"

"I was the one who got in Colleen's pretty head and planted the seed which lead ta the urn's destruction. I am the reason ye have no hope ta regain yer soul."

"And Colleen's fate? Did ye ha' a hand in that?"

A grin stretched on Cormac's face in answer.

"Damn you! Ye let Jamie take the blame for it."

"Man, he was fucking yer wife. I hardly think he was blame free. Ye forget, his appetites were something else ta be desired. Ask the priestess, she kens well, Jamie's appetites."

"What did you say?" Brenawyn asked incredulously.

"Stand and face me, coward," Alex interrupted.

"I hardly think so." With a flick of Cormac's wrist from across the room, the air became thin. "Yes,

Brenawyn, Jamie was yer husband, though ye knew him as Liam. We tracked several hopefuls in this time, ye were only one. He was assigned ta test yer abilities. When yer powers didna surface even after the beatings, and the miscarriage, he let well enough alone."

"What the fuck are you telling me, you bastard?"

"Are ye soft-heided then?" Cormac shrugged his shoulders. "I'd thought t'were obvious."

Brenawyn turned to Alex, "Did you know?"

"Kent that ye were marrit ta Jamie? Not until I saw the picture that ye tried to burn in the fireplace last night."

"And the rest?"

Alex broke eye contact with her, "Aye, I kent that ye were being watched as a potential."

"Did you watch me?"

"From time ta time. I had a duty."

"How?"

He shook his head uncomprehending, "How?"

"Yes, how did you watch me from time to time?"

"Through Leoncha, yer grandfather actually." He rubbed the back of his neck. "I inserted myself inta their acquaintances years ago. Played up the family connection of friends they already had."

Brenawyn turned to Leo, "Were you aware of this?"

"No." Leo answered stepping forth to stand by her.

Brenawyn turned back to stare at Alex. "You claim that you didn't know Liam was my husband until last night. You must not have been very good as your job if something that big slipped by you."

"Brenawyn, lass, it wasna that way. Ye ha' ta believe

101

me!" Alex pleaded. "Each bard has his own way for coercing the latent talents out of a hopeful. Individual methods have never been questioned."

"So don't ask, don't tell?"

"Brenawyn. It wasna like that.

"Tell me, Alexander, how was it then?"

"We didna ken one another till that morning at the bakery. I was only so close ta yer family as ta hear stirrings o' anything if they arose."

"Then what happened to make you change tactics?"

"The others, they had proven themselves ta be … but the prophecy and the omens still pointed ta this time. Ye were the only one remaining even though yer powers hadn't come ta the surface."

"So you knew where I'd be and you forced the introduction."

"Nay." It was Cormac who spoke. "I was one step ahead of Alex. The Oracle and I were tracking ye, and we met at the rest stop. We would ha' had ye then, but for Alex, who dropped the veil just enough ta set yer dog off."

"Why didn't you just let them take me?" Brenawyn asked Alex.

"Because by that time, I kent what they were up ta, and I couldna let them succeed."

"So you stepped in and assigned yourself the task of seeing whether I was the one. What methods did you use?"

"Brenawyn … "

"Tell me."

Alex sighed. "Much less than I was prepared to use. I didna employ the use of memory bindings. Yer memories are true."

"No, you just fucked me."

"Och, lass, nay. I only told ye stories enough ta get yer interest up. When I brought ye to the park were the Lughnasadh ceremony of thanksgiving was ta take place, it was ye who asked permission of the gods. The earth responded ta ye. I saw it, felt it. Then I was thaur during the ceremony and saw the East, West, North, and South spirits answer yer call. I brought you back to the house, and I learned that ye were possessed by not just the fertility goddesses but by all of them."

"I can confirm that at least," Leo interjected. "I was the one who figured out how to get them to release you."

"I didn't know that. Why didn't you tell me?" Brenawyn asked.

"There was so much going on, so many things happened all at once. I couldn't keep up. Then trying to explain it all?"

"How did you get them to release me?"

"Through the use of blood magic. I used my blood and his to activate all four of his spirit animals: the leopard, wolf, bear, and hawk. The essences of the gods were dispersed through their Forms."

"Ye ha' been gone for six hundred years."

She stiffened, "Explain better."

"The one destined ta be priestess was gone and each member of the Coven had ta search to the ends o' the land for signs. Aerten and Caer Ibormeith, the goddesses of fate and prophecy were consulted by the Vates' augury. Potentials were identified."

"How many?"

"In this time?"

"In all times."

Cormac answered, "Thirty-two all together."

"Thirty-two. And in this time?"

Alex found his voice, "Three."

"And their fates? Are they still alive?"

"Aye." Cormac answered.

"But neither left unscathed." Alex followed up.

Brenawyn scoffed, "Do you condone such treatment?"

"O' course, I doona. How could ye ask such a question? That's the reason I got involved with you. I couldna abide their abuse o' one more person."

"Enough. Ye may be interested in the little trick I learnt from the Oracle. She, an unwitting instructor, I ha' nonetheless become her most apt pupil."

Scarlet sigils, lit up on Cormac's arms, surprising Brenawyn. The markings covered his exposed forearms but were not connected like hers, her grandmother's, or Alex's. She didn't know he had the ability. Who was this man?

"Her craft o' augury has intrigued me from the moment I first witnessed it." He lifted his arms and spoke:

Alexander Morgan Sinclair
I claim what is yers, for my own
I quiet yer speech so ye canna call out
I silence yer tongue so ye canna plead for aid
I dull yer mind so ye canna ken what is ta come.
I say this three times, and done.

Brenawyn could see the strained cords of Alex's neck, and his jaw tense as he tried to swallow. Alex gasped for breath, his hands clutching at his throat, trying to pull an invisible bind away. Panic set in. She could see it in his eyes. She could feel it in the pit of her stomach. He was going to die again. She went to him, clueless as to what she could do to help.

"Ah, doona try ta speak … it will close yer windpipe all the further. I ha' taken yer voice. Nothing else, I assure ye. Doona believe me? Try calling out ta her."

Alex screamed a noiseless warning. He could feel his vocal cords strain, his tendons stretch. He tried again. Nothing.

"I want ye around, dae ye see, ta ken finally that thaur is nothing ye could dae ta save her. I want ye thaur when I strip her powers. I want ye ta see her torn open by the Oracle's knife. I want ye ta see her writhe in pain, ta call out ta ye in her last. And then I want ye ta be thaur when I take her abilities, and finally ascend to godhood."

Brenawyn felt Maggie at her back trying to force something in her hand. From the length and weight, she had just given her the metal meat tenderizer as Alex held Cormac's attention.

Bones lengthened and reformed. Fur sprouted and ran along his spine. He looked out of feline eyes again when the shift was complete. Cormac stood transfixed.

Timing it right, Alex's leopard pounced as Brenawyn and Maggie lifted their weapons. Cormac somehow knew they were behind him, and he swung his body to meet Brenawyn, striking her across the cheek. He took the brunt of the mallet on his shoulder, sidestepping in time to avoid a fatal blow. Alex made contact, toppling Cormac to the ground. Jaws latched onto his vulnerable neck, teeth pressing in, the carotid artery so close, heart beat increasing, the odor of stale sweat and dry urine assaulted Alex's nostrils.

Alex felt Cormac's enchantment fall when the heaviness in his chest lifted. Still as the leopard, his full senses rushed back. He could hear Brenawyn unfold herself from the heap rising up with an angelic smile across her bloodied face. She turned her attention to him, running her hand up the length of his black-furred back as he pinned Cormac to the ground. "Ah, I can see it, a beautiful thing, surrounding you. It looks so delicate ... so easily torn." Brenawyn purred.

Her sigils lit up, and an athame appeared in her hand, the same that had gutted Alex in Salem, *her* knife. The one she had said she didn't want. Its blade glowed the same as her eyes. Leo must have must have enchanted it beforehand and secreted it to her.

Alex knew what she was attempting to do, but did not know if she knew the ramifications. He tried to scream a warning to her but all that escaped his mouth was the chuff of the leopard. He couldn't take the chance of losing his hold on Cormac in the seconds it took to shift. But, if Brenawyn was successful at tearing a hole in the veil she would be exposed, vulnerable to the rest of the Coven. He would be called back to the Hunting Grounds. The act no god could ignore. It would incense the Hunters, give the sluaghs his scent; it would begin, and he could not let the

Wild Hunt through the rift. The level of destruction they would wreak would be like nothing this world had ever seen.

"Enough," she ripped at the air, a hiss, like the leaking air from a tire, so faint, could just be heard.

In the distance the baying of dogs started. Leo bent down to grab a fistful of Cormac's hair. Alex repositioned himself bracing four paws and putting his entire weight on Cormac to allow her to pick up his head so she could see recognition in his eyes. "Do you have anything left to say to us? The dogs have his scent now. It won't be long until they come for him. Do you dare to be present when they do?"

Cormac looked through the tear in the veil, and Alex imagined Cormac could see what he could. The shadows of the pack, incensed with the smell of prey, and the more ominous antlered one hanging back—the one of whom they all should be fearful.

"This is not over between us, Shaman. Once I rip her powers from her, you will be next to follow her into the unknown. Fate be damned." He sifted time and was gone.

In the same moment, Alex found his voice and the magic dispersed allowing him freedom. He shifted and Maggie threw him the sweats she retrieved from his room.

"What happened, Leoncha?"

"Go, go, get clothes on. The bags are packed, grab them. Hurry. You need to go. Take her, and run. Before the Cernunnos comes for you."

Entering again a few minutes later, Alex was fully dressed with two packs slung over his shoulder. "The

107

house, isna safe. They came. They willna stop now. Ye need ta leave too. The two o' ye 'afore the gods come. They willna be kind."

"We will take care."

"First, the rift needs ta be closed. It willna stop them from coming for me, but it will stop them from entering this realm. Brenawyn, give me the knife."

She gave it over, stepping closer interested in the proceedings. "Leo, teach her ta enchant the blade, please.

Come here, Brenawyn. You need to isolate the healing sigils. The blue of your interlace only."

"Okay. How do I do that?"

Alex interjected, "Dae ye remember what it felt like when ye healed me?"

Brenawyn felt the blush creep up her neck, "Yes."

"Focus, lass. Dae ye need a demonstration?"

"How?"

He put her hand on his chest and localized his own sigils. The red defensive ones disappeared leaving only the blue. "Dae ye feel it?"

"Yes."

"Isolate it in ye, then focus on that only.

It took a few long seconds for Brenawyn to do this, and the effort was accompanied by frustrated mutterings, but only the blue shone after a time.

"Good lass. Now, ye need to create the same motion ye used to open the veil ta close it, but in reverse. Imagine ye are trying to cut fabric with a knife."

"I'm not sure I understand."

"Tell me, Brenawyn, what dae ye see?" Alex

108

motioned to the rift. From his vantage point, he could see a section of the forest thickly covered in swirling fog. He knew what that fog felt like on his skin. Cold, damp, clinging. It distorted vision. In it, shadows moved, large impossible shadows that belonged to things not of this realm. What would she see? Could Brenawyn, if she were the priestess in truth, and not just by her word, see what no one else could? See what he could?

"I see nothing."

"Ah," he couldn't keep the disappointment from his voice, "that's good."

"But, if I take my eyes out of focus, there seems to be something ... like a spark of light, shadows where they shouldn't be, dim though, and it's like ... "

Alex grabbed her hand as she stretched her arm out to touch, "Ne'er go ta touch something ye see in the other realm, dae ye hear me?"

Brenawyn shook her head, not understanding.

"When ye are in this realm, and the veil is opened, if ye breach the divide inta the other, ye'll be sucked in."

"Oh." Brenawyn took two steps back clutching her arms to her chest. "I didn't realize."

"T'is meant ta be alluring. This is whaur the auld stories come from o' the fairie stealing children and maidens. Thaur are many things that lay beyond that are waiting."

"But you had said that nothing can hurt me in Tir-Na-Nog?"

"Aye, that I did, and inasmuch as it is, t'is true; but this is no' Tir-Na-Nog. These are the Hunting Grounds.

Haur ye will see beasties that would gi' the gods nightmares. Ye ha' shades that canna remember their former lives, even enough ta ha' a glimmer o' pity or compassion. All that controls them is their hunger. Ye ne'er want ta go haur. E'er. I ken, ye see. Take me a' my word. I ken o' what I speak."

"Okay, Alex. I believe you." Brenawyn took a firmer grip on the athame's handle. "Tell me what to do."

"From yer left hip ye need to pierce the veil and follow it up to yer right shoulder."

As she was finishing repairing the tear a horn sounded from beyond the opening, otherworldly and dark, the sound made the fine hairs on her arms stand. She faltered in her last few inches, and Alex knew that she could see the steed with glowing red eyes approach at a gallop. The rider on its back ducked and twisted for entry but stopped short of the rift, staring at her, his eyes only for her. Tattoos covered the expanse of his chest and arms, and a great antlered helm of gold encrusted with precious stones covered his head, throwing what little could be seen of his face in deep shadow. He bowed his head to her. "Daughter."

The word was uttered as an invocation of recognition. Brenawyn shivered in response and doubled her efforts to close the rift.

"Who the hell was that?"

"That was Cernunnos," Alex sighed. "We'll meet him again soon, I ken."

CHAPTER 9

The silence was deafening in the car. Guilt weighed on him. To tell her that that was the last time she'd see her grandmother and Maggie, and the dog too ... but he couldn't risk her resistance in leaving. He would bide with whatever the outcome, even if she hated him, as long as she was safe. After twenty-five miles he made a right onto Route 30 North. It was a straight run from here, though they were still an hour out.

"Where are we going?"

"Thaur," he pointed to the first of the signs advertising the Howe Caverns.

"Really?" Brenawyn turned to face him, "I haven't been there in years. Have you ever been?"

"Nay. No' ta these caves."

"But, you've been to others? In Scotland or someplace else?"

"I ha' been ta Smoo Caves in Scotland most recently. Thaur were others much more vast and more beautiful, but doona tell a Scot that last bit, lass. Aye?"

Brenawyn laughed. "I promise. I have been to Howe Caverns a couple of times because Nana lived up here obviously, but I've been to Crystal Caves in Pennsy more frequently. Liam ... " she stopped and looked out the window her anger rising. "Well, I think he liked to go there. I'd have to assume that he did. We went often."

Alex acknowledged her statement with a nod of his head hesitant to bring up anything related to that bastard, but he was splitting hairs. Their purposes were the same, just different methods to bring about the same end.

"Why would he do that?" Brenawyn asked.

He shrugged. "Maybe he just liked going thaur?"

She gave him a withering look.

"Aye, did he act peculiar when ye went?"

"He'd insist that I touch the rocks as we passed them, even though you are expected not to. There are rules that are outlined by the tour guides there. I got all kinds of looks of displeasure, but rarely anything more than that."

Alex nodded, but gripped the wheel until his knuckles were white. He sensed that she needed to talk. She would need to before long. She needed to say it aloud, what she knew now to be true. Something about doing so was the moment of acceptance, an instant in time that she would speak the Truth and know it for herself. Brenawyn needed to admit the horrible things that bastard had done to her, but Alex was not pleased about hearing them.

"He was always peculiar. Watching. Expecting.

112

Anticipating. Ugh. Was I so naïve? I must have been. So easily tricked into believing he was in love with me. That he wanted me as much as I wanted him. God, he was so … he had this … " Brenawyn balled her fists and grunted. "Gravitational pull." She looked sideways at him, "I'm sorry. You don't need to hear this."

"T'is a'richt lass. Get it off yer chest."

Brenawyn clamped her lips shut, and looked down at her lap but continued, "Women would throw themselves at him. The first time I met him was in a class we took together. I had seen him around campus, I didn't know his name, but he was a large man, hard to miss." She nodded her head, smiling slightly. "Handsome. Lord, he was attractive. I was thrilled he happened to walk into my philosophy class, and further when he sat in the back of the room next to me. Every woman in the room took notice, especially these two sitting in front of us. The weeks went by, and the heels got higher, the skirts got skimpier. It was like they were going clubbing after our ten thirty class was dismissed at noon." Brenawyn snickered, "Or to return to work their corner."

She looked out her window, her voice hardening, "One day, the twit who sat in front of me turned to him and asked if he wanted to get out of there. He looked at her, then at me, handing me the bag of chips we had been sharing, and got up to leave with her. Honestly, I thought that I'd missed my opportunity, but when I saw him next class, he behaved the same easy way."

"So why are ye telling me this, lass?"

"The other girl never came back to class. At the time,

I just took it as she had dropped, and I thought no more of her. Liam and I started dating soon after."

"Aye?"

Brenawyn nodded, "Then it happened one day, the … the violence."

"Ah, dae ye want ta tell me about it then?"

"I think that I need to. Do you mind terribly?"

"Nay, Brenawyn, I doona mind."

"I was entering the building going to class and ran into a man I knew. He was the brother of someone I went to high school with. We talked for a few minutes in the atrium. You know, catching up. We hadn't seen one another in years. I lost touch with his sister soon after we graduated. The conversation was innocent, but Liam was there waiting for me. He had to have heard the entire conversation. It wasn't that big of an entrance, a couple of chairs, a folding table with pamphlets, and a potted plant.

"I didn't even see him coming. He grabbed me so hard it rocked my head back. Rich, that was the man's name, tried to intervene, but Liam turned on him, and broke his nose. I remember thinking that there was so much blood, but Liam forced me out, dragging me. I stumbled a couple of times to the parking lot."

Alex looked at Brenawyn, her voice was strained, panicked, higher. He put the blinker on, moved over into the shoulder, and put the hazards on.

She didn't give notice but continued, "Falling to my knees, but he hoisted me up, picked me up in a fireman's hold. No one even bothered to look up. There were people there! A lot of people!"

Alex put the car in park and undid his seatbelt to turn to face her more fully.

"He slapped me. Hard. My eyes teared. I tasted blood. My cheek swelled immediately."

Alex reached for her hands, but Brenawyn pulled away.

Brenawyn was shaking, "How did I allow that to happen?"

"Brenawyn, lass."

"No, how could I have married him?"

"It was the memory bindings."

"You mean to tell me that they are that good? They are that effective to make me forget that much?"

"Aye. Nay. Only if t'was conjured by Oghma himself. Aye, he could ha' done it."

"The same god that gave me back my memories? You took me to him. What the hell were you thinking?"

"Brenawyn, wait!"

She batted away his hands, and fumbled with the door handle, sobbing.

Alex leaned over her to grasp the door handle before she bolted. "Doona go, Brenawyn. Thaur was nay way for me ta ken that the bindings were made by him or the extent that they went. Please, believe me."

The fight went out of Brenawyn, and she looked at him. "Tell me how they work."

"At its base, each binding has a hallucinogen, likely psilocybin mushrooms. They are common enough. A spell is cast ta set the effects o' the mushroom permanently or a' least for a long-term, and ta leave the mind open for

115

suggestions. Bacopa monnieri is used to decrease blood pressure, and spread calm as a simplistic memory is introduced. The mind has ta be a' rest for the memory ta take, ken? Then rosemary is always used, as well as walnuts, and perhaps a certain kind of club moss."

"Walnuts, really?"

"Aye, they are filled with a memory booster. I kin ye call it Omega-3 fatty acid."

Brenawyn looked at him, and shook her head incredulously. "Is there anything you don't know?"

"Aye, plenty, but about this, nay. I am the Reliquary. All knowledge related to the Druids, their history, customs, spells, incantations, I ken. That is my office. The knowledge has been passed down ta me by those that came before."

"That explains me, but the memory bindings also affected Nana, and I guess some others too, because no one ever noticed anything was wrong, but maybe that was part of the bindings too. I'm getting confused."

"Och, the bindings would ha' ta ha' been redone ta include Leo, possibly Maggie, and yer close friends whaur ye lived. That's what leads me ta believe that Oghma ta be the conjurer. No one else could ha' done it."

"Can you?"

"I kin the mechanics o' it. I possibly could manage one, but no' multiples."

"So what now? Where do we go?"

"That is the crux o' our problem. The circle o' trust is dwindling. Yer family, Leo, is nay guard against those that come for ye. I doona even ken the extent o' the danger. My instinct tells me ta take ye back ta my family seat. Ye'd be safer thaur."

"Safer?"

"Aye. Unfortunately, I canna guarantee yer complete safety but I can offer ye the protection o' my family and several powerful Druids who I would stake all that I hold dear, wouldna be turned."

"All right, but I'm not promising anything, either way. I don't run, but I have the God given sense to stay away from danger. What do you want me to do?"

"Go with me ta the Caverns."

"That's it?"

"For now."

They pulled back on the highway, and she reached over to put on the radio. She was done talking for now. She had to process. How would she be able to leave her grandmother? Spencer? The friends she had back in Jersey? She would be doing just that. This wasn't a move out of state, it was a death sentence for that's what those she left behind must think beyond her grandmother and perhaps Maggie. Oh Maggie, the closest thing to a sister she had. She wouldn't get to see her get married, have children, God, this was so unfair.

When was she going—to the time when the balance became *unbalanced*—could he be more vague? What the fuck was the balance anyway and how was she to restore it? Who the fuck cared? Most people just mind their own problems, their own drama, they don't care about the world, just how it affects them in their little microcosm. Shit, would he take her back to his time, six hundred years

117

ago, or further?

She wracked her brain trying to think of what the history books said about the medieval period. No antibiotics, little regard for hygiene, no plumbing, no refrigeration, no modern conveniences at all, how dependent was she on them? Why would she even have to have these thoughts, it was nothing but wild imaginings that would have her dream up these events.

Wait, was she dreaming?

Brenawyn pinched herself. She pinched herself again and again. Nothing. Shit. Perhaps she was insane? Would she know necessarily, if she was? She didn't think so.

Perhaps this was what she was meant to do.

Whoa, where the hell did that come from? But since it did, hadn't she always felt out-of-place? She always attributed that to losing her mother, then shuffled around for years until Dad's death before finally ending up at Nana's, but as lovely as she was and as good a substitute for her mother and father, she didn't feel like she belonged—always on the outside looking in.

Then Alexander Morgan Sinclair. Holy Lord. Was he not what she expected? She'd almost take a womanizer over what he was. She could have dealt with that, possibly had some fun along the way, but as it was, she the priestess and he the Shaman. To have him as her lover. Holy Lord, talk about baggage and something to seriously consider. What she wouldn't give for just a womanizer, the most that would be hurt would be her feelings, of course barring a run or two of antibiotics. But as it stood now, evisceration then death—great, wonderful, so glad she signed up.

He turned on Discovery Drive and a short while later pulled up in front of the Caverns Motel. Alex shut off the car and took a long look at her. She didn't respond. He got out to secure their stay, but when he returned, she was standing next to the car looking up into the night sky. She smiled, not turning her face to him, "Will they look the same where we are going?"

"If we were ta be in this verra spot, aye they would."

"That gives me some comfort to know the people I know and love could look up at the sky and have it be the same one I look at, despite distance and...time."

His mouth went dry, "Brenawyn, are ye sure?"

She nodded sadly, giving his hand a squeeze, and walked down the sidewalk and into their rented room.

CHAPTER 10

Alex studied the map of the cave system on the wall of the main lodge's lobby before deciding on the Signature Rock Discovery Tour. It looked to be the most comprehensive and, according to the advertisement, the new areas weren't electrified so that spelunkers would be able to see the underground system as it had originally been viewed back in the 1900's. It would give Brenawyn a chance to adjust to the complete blackness and the physical strain of spelunking that they would encounter on their second visit later that evening. He'd have to remember to stop at the gift shop afterward to purchase a cave map to include with their provisions.

He turned to find her looking in the window of the gift shop at the displayed geodes and jewelry of semi-precious stones. She was casually dressed in acceptable, even modest attire for this age, but where they were going it would be scandalous. He'd regret not seeing her legs once they went back, or any part of her natural figure. She'd be bustled in stays and paniers then swathed in layers of heavy fabric except for secreted moments, but how many would he be allowed to have? He put the thought out of his mind, disgusted with himself for allowing his yearning to enter the reality of day.

They were just waiting for the tour guide to return with the coveralls, lighted helmets, and boots, though Brenawyn passed inspection in that regard. She wore a pair of Asolo Meridians that had been waterproofed. Alex chuckled again remembering the boy's shock as it registered on his face when she told him she actually had appropriate footwear. Obviously the caves didn't have too many prepared visitors. As for himself, he gave over his shoe size also. He didn't generally require additional means of protective gear, and did not require it now if not for the need to blend in with other would-be visitors. This afternoon's foray was a reconnaissance mission to assess security and to scout out a good location for the incantation of Widdershins, the time traveling spell he would need to perform.

When the tour guide reappeared hefting a box of helmets on his shoulder and carrying a pile of neatly folded coveralls tucked under the other arm, Alex had a chance to peer into the room beyond before the door slammed shut. It had an open closet of hanging coveralls and overhead shelves for boots, each organized according to size. Helmets must be in there too on the opposite wall. There was no other place for them in the lodge. The building's structure wasn't that big, and there was no lock on the door. That would cut down last minute prep time.

The coveralls felt damp and smelled a bit musty, despite the use of strategically placed dehumidifiers throughout the space; there was no help for it. It was the entrance of a large cave system. Alex handed Brenawyn a coverall.

Brenawyn came over after dressing and stood next to Alex. "Are you ready for this? I haven't been on this tour; I'm excited that we'll be seeing more of the caves. I love this stuff. I always wondered what was beyond the dam. There's this metal chain at the end of the basic tour, well, I don't know if it's still there, it was when I last visited, but I always wondered what was beyond it."

"I suppose we will find out together, then." Alex responded.

They were gathered together for a group photo in front of the cave map. There were seven of them altogether; the others seemed friendly enough, with an air of excitement pervading the small group.

"Hello, folks. My name is Brianna and this is John." We'll be your tour guides this afternoon."

John waved and inserted the key into the elevator's control panel. "Nice to meet you. The elevator will be up momentarily and we can start our tour."

"The picture you just posed for will be available to purchase, as well as two others if you'd care to pose for them once we're down in the caves at the kiosk behind you at the end of our tour." Brianna added, the elevator doors opened behind her, "Ah, here we are!"

"I thought that the tour covered an unseen section of the caves without lights and walkways?" a middle-aged man in the group asked.

"You are correct, but the tour begins at the bottom of this elevator, and there are lights there. This will be the easiest part of today's tour because we will be on walkways and we'll see the spectacular rock formations. The various sediments, existing minerals, and species of moss in places provide vivid color. We'll be passing the photo opps and if anyone would care to take advantage … "

John shrugged his shoulders and winked in Alex's direction, nodding his head once at the protective arm Alex had around Brenawyn. "Don't worry though, most of today's tour will be in the dark, the only light provided by these." He tapped his helmet lamp. "It won't disappoint."

The elevator doors closed and the car started its descent down 156 feet to the cave floor. The temperature dropped noticeably.

"You are probably noticing the change in air temperature right about now." Brianna remarked to general consent from the group. "The caves are at a constant temperature of 54 degrees in the heat of summer and the cold of winter."

~ ~ ~

Leo watched the road as one after another commuter accelerated past her. She could feel Maggie's impatience grow as the miles ticked by until it was a physical force separating the two of them. Deaccelerating further, she dug her heels in; she wasn't going to rush to say goodbye.

Thoughts swirled in her head. What to say knowing this would be the last time she spoke to Brenawyn? She didn't need advice. No reminders of memories. They both had that. What consumed Leo was the emptiness that would be left by her departure. She could not go where Brenawyn was going. There would be no contact, no communication. There would be nothing after today.

The hours ticked by louder than before, echoing in her head until there was no room for anything else but the reverberations of the seconds slipping by on her empty heart. She swiped at her eyes, wiping tears away hastily. *Don't start crying now; you won't be able to stop.* Her breath hitched on a sigh, and her heart fluttered in her chest, jabbing pain radiated out from her lower spine, sweats, dizziness. She knew her heart was giving out. She'd make an appointment at a cardiologist after this was done, but she didn't need a doctor's diagnosis to tell her that she was dying. She knew what was at stake when she accelerated Alex's resurrection process. What choice did she have? What if they sent more acolytes? Brenawyn was vulnerable. Leo knew that she was giving up what little life she had left to ensure that Brenawyn had a protector. Someone not bound by laws and who would do what was necessary.

Her hands tightened on the wheel. *Get a grip. There are things that need to be done.* "Maggie, do you know how to drive a stick?"

"No, Leo. I never learned."

"Okay, then you take the truck back, and I'll drive Bren's car."

"Where is she going, again?"

"Scotland. Alex is taking her to Scotland at least at first."

"For how long?"

"Indefinitely … probably."

"And you're okay with this?"

"No, absolutely not, but I have no say here. She's a grown woman."

"It makes no fucking sense—sorry. I mean, why would she leave?"

"You know why, you've seen them, what they can do."

"Yes, but I've also seen what she can do, and you—what you can do, too. And Alex, I mean, what the hell? He came back from the dead, for shit's sake!"

Realizing how ludicrous the events of the past weeks must seem, Leo snorted, "You have that wrong. *We* helped him come back from the dead, for shit's sake!"

This declaration silenced Maggie, and she looked down at her hands slowly nodding her head. "Yes, I did," she whispered.

"There will be retribution, and that's why, after we tie up loose ends, we will leave too."

"Are we meeting her?"

"No, it's too conspicuous. Two people can travel faster, slip away, go into hiding. Can you imagine how much I would slow them down?"

"You're not exactly feeble, Leo."

She smiled, and reached to squeeze Maggie's hand, "No, but as a group, we'd be more recognizable, especially with the dog."

"I see why, but it still just feels wrong. It's not sitting well, here," Maggie put her hand on her abdomen.

"I understand; it feels that way for me too."

"What needs to be done when we get there?"

"Not much, other than saying goodbye." Leo simplified, eyeing the cardboard box sitting on the backseat. She knew every item in there. She had packed it herself, guessing what one would bring on such a trip. The athame and *Eiliminteach* were definites. They were two of the five pieces that were Brenawyn's by right of office. They were her rightful tools. She'd also included Margaret's journals and her grimoire. In her estimation, the journals had to be included. To so recently find out there was a physical link to her dead mother, only to lose it? The presence of the dates was unfortunate and, the possible problem they would cause if they were to fall into anyone else's hands upsetting. Though her grimoire was a greater threat, Leo wished she knew more about Brenawyn's destination. Alex was 600 years old, and if he took her back then it would be after the European witch hunts started in earnest. If the book was found in her possession, it would be enough to condemn her as a witch. When she was going, Leo couldn't foresee. It was a dangerous time, full of ignorance and fear, but she'd let Alex decide whether it was worth the risk.

~ ~ ~

Cormac paced the length of the motel, the closed doors locking him out of finding which room was theirs. Her car was here and that was enough for now. A cursory look in the window revealed nothing of note on the inside. It wasn't worth setting off the alarm. They would have to wait it out. He sent the bulk of the acolytes armed with cell phones off to scout out the area. They had watch over the main lodge, the mining building in the rear, the head of the nature trails, and key positions along the roads approaching. Alex was prepping for Widdershins. He was going to take her back. Not if Cormac had anything to say about it. He'd itched to have it done. The chase was taking too long, Samhain was approaching too quickly. He'd have to wrest her power away and claim it for his own before the next fire feast. That was the next time the veil would be thin enough to move through the realms without the expenditure of energy. He'd need to reserve all his strength for his battle with Finvarra.

The phone rang in his pocket and he touched the screen, lifting it to his ear in time to hear, "The old woman approaches from the north."

He ended the call and whistled. Another acolyte appeared at the end of the building, nodded once and disappeared. Cormac scanned the area for trace evidence of their presence, seeing none, he walked swiftly in the same direction.

He envied Alexander in moments like this. Lying in wait would be so much easier if he had the ability to shift. He'd be a bird sitting on the wire or apex of the building looking down. He'd like to see it all, even though he was impatient. He especially liked when he was successful at gaining trust. Thank the gods his pleasing face had more uses than to get a lass in the rushes. He particularly relished when their panic and fear registered followed by the rigid tension of the body, the cold sweat, and the spasmic breathing, and their faces...changing from incredulity to horror. He adjusted himself with a grunt.

Before he rounded the corner, he glanced back to see the sole picnic table directly across from the reservation office occupied by his two newest recruits. He considered the two girls, faces in their phones, and hoped that they knew the importance of what was at stake. He'd filet them himself if they were lax in their responsibility.

Before he had the chance to think further, he heard a whistle off to his right, and an acolyte extended his arm above his head palm outward, *stop.* Then a fist in a circular motion at the waist, *prepare to move. Understood.*

Interminable minutes later, Cormac watched the man pick up his phone again, nod, and make eye contact, extending his arm again holding up four fingers. *Room Four.* There was little chance they could do this next part without attracting attention, so they would just have to be quick about it.

He came around the side of the long building and sauntered to Room Four, lightly rapping his knuckles on the door. He was granted entrance immediately; there were three of his men in the room, and the women were bound and gagged huddled together on the far edge of the bed.

"Well done, lads. Well done." Cormac commented. "Secured the ladies without a clishmaclaver. Och, now I kin we can wait ta hear when the priestess emerges. Sinclair willna take her through Widdershins just yet. He needs ta scout it out first."

Cormac approached the dog and put his fist out so he'd get a scent. The dog sniffed his hand and pulled its jowls away from his teeth, emitting a low growl. The younger woman gave what he thought to be a satisfied grunt. He pulled his hand and backed away, skirting around the dog to face her. "Ye kin that funny? Dae ye?" He backhanded her. "What about now?" He turned to one of his men, "Go get the Vate. She needs ta prepare."

A few minutes later, the Vate came in escorted by the acolyte with an arm under hers for support. She leaned into him heavily, her breathing labored. She smacked her lips together, wheezing. "Dae ye ha' what is needed?"

"Aye. E'verything that ye asked for is haur in the bag."

"Good. Lay them out for me."

The Vate grabbed the knife and approached the old woman, seizing a handful of her hair. Both women reacted and tried to push her away, but the acolytes were on them and the Vate resumed her progress. She sawed at a lock of Leoncha's hair, close to the root. Turning her attentions to Maggie, she snatched at one of the many piercings the girl had in her ear lobe. It didn't take much force to rip it from her ear, punctuated by a muffled scream. Maggie pivoted her body away rolling on the injured ear, but the Vate was there, a lithe strength belying her first appearance in the room. She put a knee on the girl's abdomen and her gnarled claw forced her chin around exposing the bleeding lobe once again. She clucked as she gathered a handkerchief to wipe at the blood. The acolyte went to pin her to the bed, but was stayed by the Vate.

MELISSA MACFIE

"Nay, doona dae that. The incantation will work that much better if she has piss and vinegar ta her, and I'll ha' a better chance o' getting what was taken from me returned."

Taking the hair and the bloody handkerchief to the pile of supplies, she put them aside and lit the sage bundle letting the smoke permeate the room. She lay that aside in an incense holder, and turned again to the specimens she had procured from the women.

"The bluid is necessary. It should be from someone who is related, but as long as I ha' a token from a relative," holding up the hair, "t'will serve. T'was a surprise that she was able ta bind my powers, even the gods didna see that. That's why she is so important. Nothing can be gleaned from her or what she is capable o' beyond the events that ha' more ta dae with others than her. She'll come inta her powers fully after she gives birth, though whose going ta sire it, Aerten and Caer Ibormeith doona ken either."

Leo tried to launch herself off the bed, but was restrained by her jailor.

The Vate cackled. "Dae ye still kin ye can dae anything ta stop this?"

Leo grunted through the gag.

"Aye, ye are shortsighted then. She was ne'er yers. Ye need ta gi' o'er. I'll ha' my powers restored shortly, and ascend ta Oracle once more, then we can proceed."

The Vate put the hair in the opened handkerchief and hocked up phlegm from a deep wet cough and spit it into the midst of the fabric square, rubbing it in with her thumb. She laid it down on the carpet, squatting over it. "I will say it so ye can kin the truth and cower 'afore me and what is ta be.

"Hear me, oh dark artisans o' Falias, Gorias, Murias, and Finias. Long ha' ye waited in the shadows. Grant me the sight once more. Grant me what has been taken again. I beseech ye, let me be the herald o' the old ways, the days o' yer rule. I ask this in the name o' Addanc, Badb, Neit, Ratis, Taliesin, and ... Mandred."

Leo screamed through the gag, shaking her head while tears ran down her cheeks.

CHAPTER 11

Alex and Brenawyn left the main lodge from the back exit and processed up the steps to the mining building. She had mentioned that she wanted to see the machine that cut geodes, and while he'd readily granted her request, the growing anxiety in his heart would not let him be. She talked pleasantly, and he must have answered in kind, but his mind whirled. He was taking her back. She was not ready; her life here hadn't prepared her. How would she fare without modern conveniences?

After watching the wet saw cut its way through a geode through the safety of the glass window, she was the one who had suggested they walk the nature trails. Soon he found himself leaving the manicured hills and entering sparse forest, but the evidence of man was still present. Someone had come recently to try to cut back the encroaching wilderness. Beyond this, the trees were larger, older, and the undergrowth was tangled. They were in the reserve. The birds whistled in the trees and animals scurried about underneath the canopy far away and sometimes close by, startling Brenawyn from time to time. He heard her gasp and pick up her pace momentarily only to fall back into her plodding steps moments later. He could hear her behind him huffing with effort, but not one word of complaint. Good. He wasn't prone to rest now that she was set on the task at hand.

While he waited for her to catch up, none too concerned that the noise she was making would scare away any game within ten miles. After all this wasn't a hunting trip.

"Dae ye need a rest?"

"No thank you. You have a longer stride than I do though. Slow your pace so I can keep up."

"Noted. T'is no' much further. Ha' ye e'er been haur?"

"Not here, no. But near here yes."

"Ta the falls?"

"Depends. I've been to several, but not all of them."

Some treacherous footing brought them to a moss covered outcropping, a center seat to watch water cascade from a precipice fifty feet above. He turned to see Brenawyn stopped a few feet back, mouth slightly ajar, staring. She dropped the bag, rushed over and gave him a kiss full of promise, or so he imagined, and let her tow him over to the center of the small clearing. There, a tug on his arm had him kneeling to settle next to Brenawyn, who had dropped to sit on the ground, her legs folded to the side.

She leaned into him placing her hand on the thigh of his outstretched leg. His heart gave a leap in response to his own physical reaction to her nearness—he was a boy again, holding his first girl.

He'd willingly sit here forever, wholly distracted by the scent of lavender clinging to the tendrils of her hair, the swell of her breast visible above the shirt's neckline, or the curve of her hip pressed against his own. It took all his thoughts to corral the urge to press her down and bury himself within her.

"It's so beautiful," she whispered. He agreed, placing a kiss on the crown of her head, gladdened that she didn't see that he wasn't referring to the falls.

"Whaur we are going the forest is much denser. T'is no' safe in any time ta travel through the forest in the dark, too many dangerous spots, take a few steps off the path and ye could find yerself at the bottom o' a ravine with a broken leg or worse. "Haur gi' the pack ta me."

She handed it over and watched him take out food stuffs. He wrapped it up in a small bag, tied a rope to it and swung the rope lasso style up over a high tree limb. After hoisting it up and securing the rope, he came back. "In case of a roaming bear."

"A bear?" Brenawyn looked around as if she expected a bear to pop out from behind a bush.

"Relax. T'is just what one does when sleeping out o' doors, a precaution; larger animals tend ta stay away. Strange smells. The precaution is more for raccoons that would scavenge the site in the matter o' minutes. We'll be returning ta the inn soon, but I'd gi' ye a crash course in survival."

"Survival Skills 101," she laughed. "Okay. Now what?

Digging in the pack, Alex found the roll of twine. "Dae ye kin how ta set a snare trap?"

Thoroughly amused, Brenawyn answered, "No, I never had cause to learn."

"I'll teach ye then. First, ye ha' ta leuk for branches low ta the ground that ha' enough spring in them. This one is good." Alex bent it. "Then ye take a length and secure it ta that branch, like this."

Brenawyn nodded, interested.

"Then ye need ta find another sturdier branch about so big," holding his fingers about a foot apart. "And cut yerself a notch in it, or sometimes yer lucky enough ta find one that has grown like that naturally." He broke it off a fallen log and returned. With the knife he dug a hole and secured an end of the stick a few feet away. "Now, ye'll need ta attach the two with the twine, and tie a small noose ta lay on the ground in front of it." Alex finished the trap, and sat back on his haunches. "This trap is the easier one ta set, and it will get ye game with much more frequency, but the quarry will be small, rabbits, squirrels, birds, and the like." Alex stood leaving the snare.

"You're not going to leave that, are you?"

"Not feeling like turkey tonight? Or is it the prospect o' cleaning it that has ye worrit?

"Um, if that were to happen, I wouldn't be cleaning it."

"Don't worry, lass. I would be doing it, but ye ne'er

ken when a skill will be needed."

"Actually, it wasn't that I didn't have the opportunity to learn in my early years, I was raised on a farm with no pets except for those I found in the barnyard. I had two chickens as pets; they would follow me around, wait for me to come home from school. I was there when they hatched, raised them from chicks. But times got tough, I think, after my mom died, though I was young so I couldn't be sure, and the chickens were the last to go, as meals that is."

"Ah, lass, he should ha' no' let ye keep them from the start."

"Well regardless, one day I came home from school and called to my chickens but only the one answered. I looked and looked abandoning my school books by the back door, never in my mind entered the thought to check inside. I had finally given up, my insides empty, tear streaks dried on my face when I finally entered and the first thing I saw was my Natasha, lying on the butcher block counter waiting to be plucked. My father waiting for me arms crossed at the kitchen table. I screamed at him, the first and really the last time I did, ran past him, up the stairs to my bedroom. I stayed in there a long time. He tried to come in once, but I barred the door, jamming a chair underneath the doorknob. After that a soft knock a bit later. When I eventually came down it was two days later, a plate of chicken and potatoes sat on the floor just outside my room. I remember looking at it for a long time. Eventually, I picked it up and went downstairs. My father was in the kitchen, his head in his hands. I don't think he heard me at first, because it was only when I slammed the refrigerator door balancing what was left of the chicken in my arms did he look up. I didn't say a word, but proceeded outside and after getting a shovel from the shed, dug a grave for my Natasha.

My father was waiting on the stoop when I approached and he reached out to touch my arm and I shrugged him off but rounded on him again, I think he thought I was going to strike him, but I scooped up Nastralia, my other bird, and just said, 'Never again.'

Shortly after that, he allowed Nana to come visit, and two years after that, I found him dead at the kitchen table, his head in his arms."

"Och Brenawyn, *a chuisle*, I didna mean …I just thought … ye had such a sad childhood. I'm so sairy."

"I know. It wasn't all bad. Relax. It's okay. I only meant that to leave the trap would be cruel when the intent wasn't for food."

Alex nodded his understanding. "What o' building a fire?"

"Ah, well, I haven't much practice since I was in the Girl Scouts when I was ten, but I don't think the skills leave. The patience perhaps, but not the skill."

"T'is a lesson in patience ta be sure, especially with damp tinder."

A rustle drew their attention as an explosion of brush showered the edge of the clearing in leaves and small branches. The beating of hundreds of wings against leaves led the cacophony of fauna fleeing the area. Spencer burst through the trees making a beeline for her.

"Spencer! What are you … "

Alex put a hand over her mouth, "Hold yer wheest."
"Thaur," pointing to a tree across the ravine with low
hanging branches, "Can ye climb a tree?"

"I … yes, I haven't done it since I was a kid. But yeah,
if the branches are low enough."

"Just high enough ta get some cover." Assessing her
gear, "Leave the backpack and the dog. We'll come for
ye."

He stood ready for battle and the dog edged back.

Alex pushed Brenawyn in the direction from which
they came, "Go! Run! I'll give ye time. *Hurry.*"

Brenawyn looked at him for a moment, then turned
and fled.

He watched as she hit the tree line and disappeared.
He backed up to the edge of the clearing protecting her
retreat. He could see in his mind's eye the trees butted up
against the stream so the only spot she'd be out in the open
was when she crossed it. No help for that, she'd know
enough to create the smallest target, and then be in the
trees again.

If the dog were here it could mean one of two things,
though he couldn't imagine that Leo or Maggie would try
to find them this way. There was still cell phone reception
here, so really there was only one explanation. The Coven
was here.

As if the thought conjured him, out of the tree line
sauntered Cormac, inappropriately dressed in a three-piece
suit and wingtips, followed by the hunched form of the
Vate.

Neither the Vate nor Cormac made a move to go for Brenawyn, which was odd. It gave him pause, but the more pressing issue interrupted, why hadn't he sensed the danger? They were upwind of him, damn it, and with the noise of the waterfall he wouldn't have heard anything. Why didn't he think of that before choosing their location? He was slipping—he was going to get Brenawyn killed.

He took up a defensive position, bones lengthening, muscles thickening, he dropped down on his hands and knees. Before the fur of his bear had fully sprouted, he stretched his neck and roared. The Vate was at the tree line, Cormac behind him, several acolytes scattered. They were circling him, each with a dragging gait.

Alex launched himself at the nearest acolyte. The man tried to stand his ground, opened his mouth to scream, but his throat was ripped out. The second and the third man met the same end in a bloody heap, but the rotation around the clearing was complete and by the time Alex had reached its edge, all Cormac had to do was step outside the bounds of the circle he made in the dirt with his dragging step. Alex hit an impenetrable wall. Seething at his own error, Alex reared up on his hind legs towering over Cormac, the wicked claws sparking along the wall of the barrier. Beyond an ear-piercing screech and a spectacular visual it was all inside the bubble. He was caged … an impotent predator. How had he missed what Cormac was doing?

"Like that? Dae ye ken what the best part is? Hmm?" He turned and called out in Alex's voice, "Brenawyn, t'is a'richt lass. Come out."

Alex slashed at the barrier once, twice, a third time. Sparks rained down on his shoulders to vent his frustration because he knew that she'd come out of hiding, knowing nothing else. He'd have to sit here, seething as Cormac was allowed to do whatever he wished to her, unable to do anything.

"Could that be her splashing across yon stream?"

Alex whipped back to look. "

"Och, t'is. Ye are so predictable. Sending her off inta hiding by herself. This is part o' the reason ye werena meant for Shaman. So predictable, a smart enemy always has the edge."

Brenawyn emerged from the trees and crouched. The green iridescence of her eyes the only indication that she was prepared.

"Ye may no' want ta dae that, priestess." Cormac looked to the Vate, and the bound and gagged forms of Maggie and Leo, each guarded by a hooded acolyte. "Ye'll ken that the Oracle was denied ye last time we met. Ye'll no' want ta anger her further."

Brenawyn scanned the scene and made a decision. She stood, dropped her bag, and approached the Vate, the least threatening of the two. She had bested her before, perhaps she would be able to do so again. But just in case, she stopped just out of reach of the old woman.

The Vate gave a gap-toothed smile. "Aye, that's it, my bonny lass. Ye ha' some sense in yer heid. Come ta me."

"No, thank you. I am fine right here."

Brenawyn side-stepped, moving closer to Leo and

Maggie.

The Vate turned, "Cormac, bring her ta me."

Brenawyn saw the chance and jumped at Maggie's jailor, the heel of her palm jabbed at his nose. There was a satisfying crunch, and blood spurted.

Maggie turned exposing her bound wrists, and Brenawyn opened the penknife that she'd held hidden in her hand and sawed at the thick, seasoned rope. Cormac was there before she had the chance to make any headway. He grabbed a handful of her hair and wrenched her backward. Maggie glanced back over her shoulder and they made eye contact for a moment.

"Ah, priestess. Dae no' struggle. I will make yer passing quick. Yer acquainted with the Oracle."

The Oracle drew close studying her. "Ye'll remember I kin that last time we met ye took something from me. I was sore lost without it for a time, but the gods ha' decided ta reinstate my gifts that ye stripped from me. So all o' yer work was for naught."

She grabbed Brenawyn's arm, and inhaled sharply, eyes springing open. She transferred her hands to Brenawyn's abdomen kneading it. "Who did ye play the whoor for, dearie? Whose bairn dae ye carry?"

Cormac pulled on her hair making her arch her back, her face and neck exposed to him. "I ought ta kill ye now for causing so much trouble."

"Cormac Domhnall MacBrehon, we need ta wait. We canna dae this now. She is with child. She canna be touched yet."

"But ... "

141

"Nay. I ken ye are eager, as am I, ta be done with it, but remember the prophecy. She will come inta her power after ... "

"Aye, that I dae remember, but are ye sure? She doesna ha' the roundness."

The Oracle lifted Brenawyn's breasts, weighing them considering, disregarding the visceral objection that Brenawyn made at being handled that way. "Aye, t'is as I ha' said it ta be. Her breasts are heavy in anticipation."

"But if we were ta wait, then Samhain ... "

"Aye, she willna be delivered by the fire feast. We must watch her carefully, allow her ta undergo the final rite and then after she delivers, take what we need."

"And Sinclair? He willna be a hindrance?'

"Leave him ta me, Master Bard." A knife appeared in the Oracle's hand, and she ripped at the air. "The Hunt will occupy him for a time."

A horn sounded, the same low otherworldly call that Brenawyn had heard before, but this time the dark steed with glowing red eyes hurtled through the rift. The rider on its back ducked and twisted for his helm, but pulled up rein in front of Brenawyn. Tattoos covered the expanse of his chest and arms and the same antlered helm of gold covered his head. Even at this close distance, his face was shadowed. Cernunnos had arrived.

He considered her for a moment, bowed his head and turned the horse toward the circle that held Alex prisoner. He but touched it and the containment spell was broken.

Alex felt his bones shift. He fell to his knees and bowed low even before the shift had fully taken place, but he could see the sluaghs come through the rift, padding around him to make a new perimeter, boxing their prey in. The horse's razored hooves stepped close to Alex's kneeling form and pawed the ground. He could feel it breathing on his neck, and it took all his strength not to cower. He knew what those hooves felt like, trampling him the one time. He was not up to reliving the memory. "Please, Cernunnos, I humbly ... "

"Ye will dae nay such thing, prey. Long have I waited for ye ta bring me word. Longer ha' I sought ye. Now ye will answer with yer life."

"No."

All assembled turned their heads in the direction of Brenawyn's voice. "No, you will not take him." Five colors of iridescent runes glowed under her skin. Alex looked around, the horse and the hounds stared at her.

She skirted past the horse, touching it briefly on its neck. The horse shuddered in response. Cernunnos dismounted, taking a step toward her but she kept an eye only for Alex. She gained his side and only after looking at him to assess if there was any damage did she turn back to the god. "We seem to be at an impasse."

"How dae ye suggest we compromise?" asked the god.

"Give him something to cover himself as we negotiate." She left Alex's side to walk the perimeter of the circle, touching each dog on the head and flank, and each in response lay down and closed its eyes, content.

In shock, Cernunnos said, "My hounds doona sleep. They are forever on the hunt."

143

"Huh. Before this, perhaps. Let them sleep."

"I will ha' ye know that I canna stay the hunt." Cernunnos walked to his horse, and pulled a length of fabric from one of the saddle bags. "Now that he has been found he will be hunted. T'is no' only me that hunts. The others: a more insatiable lot ye'll no' find. No reasoning with them." He unraveled it, and tossed it to Alex, who in turn swathed his naked hips. "T'is beyond my control, but perhaps I can provide a temporary reprieve, though he needs ta come back with me as prisoner."

"That doesn't sound to me like a ... "

"Silence. He will remain untouched until ye come ta claim him. Ye must make yer own way thaur though, with no help from others. Ye ha' until the eve o' Samhain."

Brenawyn was by Alex's side now, and he grabbed at her wrists bending her down to plead with her. "Ye canna come for me. This is Cernunnos; he'll no' let ye go once he kens who ye are and if ye get thaur he will for sure ken it. Stay away, lass. Stay away. I canna bear it if anything were ta happen ta ye."

She touched his cheek and smiled. Brenawyn stepped out of his arms and turned to Cernunnos. "Tell me of this prison. How will he be treated?"

"He will be kept in a room lavish in its furnishings in my own home—under surveillance of course, fed delicacies..."

"Aye, ta make me fat and slow. Easy prey for yer hounds ta take down."

"Silence." Cernunnos turned to address Brenawyn again, "Fed delicacies until such time that he will be

144

rejoined with the hunting grounds."

"No harm shall come to him until then?"

"Ye have my word."

"I'll need a bit more than that, I think. Give me your hand."

"Brenawyn!" Alex and Cormac spoke up in unison, shocked at the implications.

"Nay, Brenawyn, doona," Alex repeated, but before either he or Cormac could move she slashed the penknife across her palm and did the same to Cernunnos, touching the open wounds together.

The surrounding woods grew fuzzy, I tried to blink away the blur, bringing my hand up to rub at my eyes. The movement was slow. My head felt heavy. My heart fluttered in my chest. There was another heartbeat, stronger, all around me, beating in my ears, on my body. Muffled noise distorted further. Rhythmic. Chanting. A woman's voice. Calling on someone, calling on her gods pleading ... for release. The beating grew louder, thundered in my head, my own raced to match it. Pressure building, I wanted to scream, but didn't know how. A soft almost, imperceptible sound like a soap bubble bursting, then the pressure was gone, the first joyous inhalation after release, the exaltation of riding a deluge of no pain, no pressure. Floating.

Another woman's voice at a far greater distance calling me. I didn't want to go. There were new sounds, sounds of wonder. Answers to questions I didn't know I had somewhere here in the pulse of existence, but her voice kept calling to me. Plaintively weeping. I could make her pain go away if only I went to her. The cosmos called to me too, offering the lure of knowing all, seeing all, joining with the omnipotent. But her call echoed through the infinite, and I turned my head toward it.

The surroundings snapped back into focus, leaving Brenawyn alert and aware. She reached up to touch Cernunnos' cheek. "Once I find Alexander we will discuss the terms of my servitude … *Daddy.*"

The god covered her hand with his own, visibly shaken, "Daughter, time is in short supply. The thundering hooves o' the Hunt come. I must return lest they be loosed upon yer world. I will send what help I can."

"You would leave me defenseless here with them?" Brenawyn indicated the Oracle and Cormac with a tilt of her head.

Cernunnos clapped his hands, and time stopped. Brenawyn looked around, everyone in the clearing stood motionless. Beyond, birds, insects, leaves falling from the trees had stopped too, like a painting on a canvas, so realistic, that she wandered to a nearby bush to look closer at a sparrow that had alighted. She touched its chest with the back of her knuckle, and the softness of its feathers gave to her slight touch. She gasped and went to a nearby honey bee, its wings frozen as it had prepared to lift from the head of the wildflower. She studied it intensely, never before having the desire to look at one so closely. She had spent her most of her life avoiding them, afraid she'd be stung, and sent into anaphylaxis. Now she could look without fear, see how beautiful it was with veined gossamer wings that looked insufficient to lift its fuzzy striped abdomen.

"That's a useful tool," she said when she straightened.

"It is the essence of sifting time. Ye'll learn."

"So what now?"

"Needed moments ta call for aid. I will call for Finvarra, our High King, who I will charge with keeping ye safe, along with Aerten and Caer Ibormeith."

"The goddesses of fate and prophecy?"

Cernunnos nodded his head. "I see that yer education has begun."

"Alex mentioned them not too long ago."

"Their advice is often sought, though more now than in the past. Thaur is a tension, a strain, a sense o' settling in for the task at hand, 'afore the battle."

"Let me guess, the balance?"

"Ah, so ye ken it."

Brenawyn sighed, "I've heard too much about it, and then not nearly enough."

"Lots chosen, sides taken, the war is about ta begin."

"Call who you will. I have a need to get this done."

It didn't take long before three more arrived. A man and two women, similarly dressed in white flowing robes as if it was their intention, so alluring and fair, it made Brenawyn's heart ache. The women she knew to be Aerten and Caer Ibormeith but she didn't know which was which. One had no eyes, the other had no mouth, but the absence didn't detract from their beauty.

Cernunnos said, "Let them touch ye, daughter. T'is their way o' greeting."

They gravitated toward her, each touching her on the

heart, lips, eyes, and forehead, and then bowing in turn. Brenawyn returned the gesture, to which the blind one giggled.

Finvarra was the one who spoke, "Priestess, they would ask permission ta touch ye further. Will ye grant it?"

"I … I guess so," responded Brenawyn.

It was the mute one that approached again, to take hold of her hand, giving it a squeeze of reassurance, and then placed the other on Brenawyn's abdomen. Her eyes grew wide, clouded over, and she began to convulse. Brenawyn reached out pulling the goddess to her to offer support. She eased her down and rolled her to her side as the seizure continued.

"What are ye doing, priestess?"

"I had a student once who had epilepsy. She had a seizure once in my class. It was much the same. All I could do was make sure she didn't hit her head, and didn't swallow her tongue—not much help in this case, but I remember the nurse turning her to her side when she got there. There wasn't much to do after that other than wait for the EMTs. The rest of the students moved all the desks out of the way, and we just sat on the floor with her. The seizure subsided. I felt the tension leave her body. She wept then, I don't know if it was out of embarrassment that she had an episode in school, or relief that she wasn't alone when it happened. God, it scared the hell out of me."

Her blind twin knelt down next to Brenawyn, reaching out to hold the hand of her sister. "Caer had a prophecy revealed ta her concerning ye, priestess. And yer gracious selflessness has proven a great indicator in this. For ye ken, prophecy is enigmatic, open ta interpretation based on the motives o' mortals and gods alike. Ye are plain."

She turned to Brenawyn, and even though she could not see her, she knew the goddess was seeing deeper. "Thank you?" not knowing how to respond to her last statement.

"Ye are without deception, so unlike yer kind. Ye'd act the same regardless o' situation."

"I'm predictable, I know."

"Ye say that if t'is a curse."

"Isn't it, though?"

"Ah, I kin what ye mean, but this is nay game of love, though love is involved. Ye are fair, as all great arbitrators. That will serve ye in the times ta come, priestess. Rely on that trait, as others will surely dae."

"So how does my penchant for being fair play into interpreting prophecy?"

Thaur is nothing which she cannot be
The guardians of the five will be called
And give over gladly that which has been protected.
For All hope lies with her.

"Jesus, I hate verse."

Aerten ignored her comment. "T'is nay great help, mind ye, but it does offer more o' a slant ta one side over the other. Enough ta proceed with caution in a direction, but at least thaur is a direction ta be gleaned."

149

"What is the prophecy then?"

Th' destiny o' hope from the day,
Sleeping, waiting, innocent until wha' may.
So Chance and Choice intertwined th' fates o' those
*   famed,*
To be rejoined and set right when legacy is reclaimed.

I ha' erstwhile seen this woman taken and made with
*   child,*
By th' Reliquary o' the Druid sect, a man made wild.
'Afore she kent wha' her Choice would mean,
Her strength rooted in compassion, victory be
glean'd.*

Th' Woman blessed until th' day two shall be made
*   one,*
Her powers unfulfilled until the birth is done.
Only then when hope seems lost,
Will all recognize at wha' cost.

Will the Woman prevail if all is as it seems
And defeat all machinations and schemes?
Choices must be made again for the good of all,
She must go back to the start of the fall.

I ha' erstwhile seen her turn and defeat the faceless
*   foes,*
Those that hide in the shadows waiting for the terror
*   that flows.*

For the chaos and carnage to begin,
All rests with her, whate'er her decision will fin.

"Oh Jesus Christ! Why did I ask?" Brenawyn exclaimed. Movement caught her eye. She looked over, and saw a leaf drift to the ground.

"Time grows short. I canna hold it much longer. I need ta take the Shaman back and close the rift 'afore the Hunt arrive," spoke Cernunnos.

Aerten stood, "A second needs ta be named then. The Shaman is my retribution on she who defiles prophecy."

"Let it be me, then." Finvarra's visage glimmered and gleaming armor chest plate and greaves and chainmail subramalis replaced the silken robes of moments before. A sword was sheathed on his back, and a long bow slung over a shoulder.

"As ye will, but see ta it that she does nay walk off this field."

"As ye command, so it shall be done."

Aerten approached Brenawyn again touching her on the heart, lips, eyes, and forehead in farewell. She gave Caer her hand, and the goddess regained her feet and bowed to Brenawyn, which she returned.

Cernunnos hesitated, but at last went to dig in his horse's saddle bag. The sunlight glinted off the jewelry he held in his outstretched hands when he returned. "This is yers by right. One of the five foci belonging ta the priestess. I gi' it ta ye as priestess and as my daughter ta wear. T'will help ye focus. Ne'er let it out o' yer possession." He secured it on her head.

151

Brenawyn's hand went to it immediately. A diadem fit for the pages of a Tolkien novel, she felt utterly ridiculous wearing it, but left it in place nonetheless. With that, Cernunnos clapped his hands again and time resumed. The hounds were the last to go, following Alex who looked one last time over his shoulder at her. Brenawyn stood there for a long time contemplating where she should go. What would happen if she followed them through? But logic stayed her; she didn't know what she'd be walking into, no plan, and no real ability to use her skills. She didn't even know what she was capable of. She turned to survey the camp, feeling bereft that she was without him. Cormac, the Oracle, and the retinue of remaining acolytes blocked clear passage to Leo and Maggie.

Brenawyn's attention was drawn to the clatter behind her. Finvarra slid one of his arrows from his quiver. Sight and sound blended together. The twang and reverberation of the string, the sway of the shaft, and the blur of the red tail feathers aimed at the nearest acolyte. A gasp across the clearing, and a stiff arm barring intrusion, but the arrow struck true. Finvarra shot five more in rapid succession each found their home buried in the chest of the remaining acolytes.

Brenawyn sensed the space behind her.

"T'is yer turn, priestess, a test o' yer mettle. Dispatch the Oracle."

"But … "

"She will kill ye and yer babe as soon as she can. Show no mercy."

The Oracle was advancing, sigils glowing on her skin. The humidity in the air was gone in an instant, the hot, dry, air crackled with static electricity. She reached in to her voluminous robe and pulled out a handful of dirt, and spit a wad of phlegm into it, packing it like a snowball.

"Hell, no, lady. You tried that on me before, did you forget the outcome of that? There's no way I'm letting you near me with your mudball."

Brenawyn wracked her brain, but the image that kept coming to mind was the construct that Nimue had created, not sure of how it worked, praying that the mental image was enough, she slammed her hands onto the ground. Pressure built and pushed against the dry surface and her hands, then what she thought to be tiny roots slithered against her palms, caressing her fingertips. She fought back the urge to recoil and doubled her efforts thinking about the construct. Alex had said anyone with a modicum of power could raise constructs. She hoped that by creating it she'd pass Finvarra's test and then he'd step in with the Oracle.

The ground rumbled at her feet and cracked in a wide semicircle, water from an underground source welled in the opening maw, mixing with the dirt and clay. She squatted slamming her hands on the packed earth; a reverberating thump answered her, sending ripples along the surface of the still water. A hand emerged, two, three, a dozen, spread evenly around her. Earth constructs scaled the rim, more clamored up behind the first line to stand as a wall protecting Brenawyn, but she couldn't see her adversary. Repositioning her feet for balance, she adjusted her center of gravity as the ground underneath her feet moved upward. She rose, even knowing she would become a target. When her head cleared the line of constructs and she could see the Vate, she loosed her weapon, bringing her open hand up, an opalescent orb appeared, stopping the magic-laced projectile mid-air.

Finvarra froze behind Brenawyn, and then cocked another arrow on the bow, this one aimed for her. With a crooked smile playing on his lips, he whispered, "Let's see about yer focus and observation."

She heard the twang of the string as the arrow was let loose. Brenawyn turned slightly, her other hand snatching the arrow from the air mere inches from her breast and tossed it to the ground disinterested. "What the hell are you doing?"

The Oracle's interlace grew brighter and she started chanting as the constructs advanced on her position.

I curse ye, priestess
In the name o' Belanus, god o' healing
May he turn his face from you.

I curse ye, priestess
In the name o' Epona, goddess o' fertility
May she not hear yer silent empty-armed suffering.

I curse ye, priestess
In the name o' Danu, goddess o' the land
May ye never find a home.

I curse ye priestess
In the name o' Taranis, god o' the dead.
May ye live forever.

I curse ye, priestess
In the name o' Cernunnos, god o' the hunt
May ye never find what ye seek.

I curse ye, priestess
In the name of Blodevweld ...

The chant was broken as the first of the constructs gained her position. The Oracle managed to ward off their first frontal assault with their earthly dark blades obtained from the bowels from whence they came.

Brenawyn was tiring; she grunted with frustrated effort when she felt the constructs lose solidity and one after another revert to their former state at the Oracle's feet.

"Yer focus is satisfactory. This is the end of yer first lesson," said Finvarra.

Brenawyn's chest heaved and exhaustion crept in. The bright pink orb and tendrils of blue fingers floated in front of her hand reminiscent of electrostatic generators she remembered from her high school physics lab. She dropped her hand to get a better look at it but the orb disappeared sending the projectile whizzing past her ear, as if it had just been thrown.

"Stand down. Yer exhaustion is palpable. The lesson is complete." He crossed his arms obviously impatient at her slow intake.

"You'll attack me again," Brenawyn heaved.

He waved a hand and the last of the constructs lost their solidity, mud splashed the ground, water leached out, and a thick layer of dirt lay over the ground. The last to go was the mound on which Brenawyn stood, one second solid under her feet, the next gone. She landed sprawled on her back, the painful impact knocking her out of breath.

He stood over her, "Stand down. Aye, I did attack ye, but only ta see how far yer focus reached. I ne'er meant any

harm ta come ta ye. Besides, ye are nay match for me, mortal." Then he strode to the Oracle and without preamble crushed her windpipe.

CHAPTER 12

The tightness in Brenawyn's chest and the throbbing of her lower back eased in increments until she was able to sit up.

"Mmhumuph!" From across the way her grandmother grumbled and gesticulated, as much as could she while having her hands tied behind her back.

Brenawyn closed her eyes, giving her stomach time to settle as the clearing gyrated in lopsided circles. When she ventured to open her eyes again, the clearing was spinning more slowly and it didn't seem as if she was going to vomit up the remains of her breakfast. After a few more minutes of sitting still she stretched out her legs to ease the pinpricks she felt there.

Finvarra leaned against the side of the tree from which he had emerged thoughtfully considering her. "Visions, glamours, constructs, shields. I am intrigued."

"Yeah, I'm full of surprises." She rolled her eyes, uninterested in discussion with this crazy son of a bitch, god or no. She climbed to her feet, her shaky legs felt like rubber, and looked across the clearing. Her grandmother, still bound and gagged, was sobbing. Spencer had his head on her lap. Her stomach dropped. Where was Maggie? Cormac?

Panic rose in her throat and she turned on the god. "Where's Maggie? Did that son of a bitch take her?" She strode toward her grandmother, penknife out already.

Freed of the gag now, "I couldn't stop him." Leo cried, struggling with her binds.

Brenawyn knelt behind Leo, sawing at the rope that bound her hands. She spoke to Finvarra, "And you didn't stop him?"

"Should I have?"

"Yes, damn it, you should have!"

"I dispatched the Vate as tasked."

"Nana, do you know where he took her?" She looked down at Leo's wrists, irritated and bloody, her hands swollen and purple.

"I don't know, Brenawyn. He didn't say anything. He didn't even look in my direction. He looked scared though." She rotated her shoulders.

Brenawyn kneaded a shoulder blade holding the arm out straight. Leo grunted. "I'm sorry, Nana, that this hurts." She moved to the other side to do the same, holding her lower forearm careful of her bloated hands.

"He took her as insurance. Her presence will compel ye ta follow through and go back."

Brenawyn helped Leo up. They traipsed through the woods slowly back to the Caverns Motel and while the heavy canopy overhead sheltered them from the heat of the day, it was muggy and rough going. The brush was thick and in it lay hidden holes and roots to twist an ankle or worse. If Finvarra was following, he wasn't making any noise. It was just as well. She couldn't do more than one thing now anyway. She had to get her grandmother to the relative safety of the motel at the very least.

They followed the dog, stepping where he stepped for easier going. A pounding in Brenawyn's ears began like the beat of her heart, but soon became blinding. She stopped, holding her head in her hands, doubled over. The sound of the forest, her grandmother wheezing, and the jingling of the dog's collar all drowned out.

She lifted her head to find she was in the woods of Tir-Na-Nog. The trees were the same but the light was different, shifting in different patterns when it touched the wings of the dryads. She must have been called here. She straightened and her head cleared. Looking back, she couldn't see Nana or Spencer. This was a forced crossing perhaps that was why her head hurt so much. Finally, the headache dissipated and she began walking along the path ahead of her, since she had no clear marker for which way to go. If she had been brought here, then whomever had done it would ensure that she find the right path.

After only a few yards the Wolf emerged and joined her, whining, crying as he approached. She patted its side when he fell into step with her; she felt like crying too. The Wolf leaned into her and she stepped to the side. So he was

159

her guide. "All right, lead on, my furry friend."

She put a hand on his back and felt the subtle shifts of the direction change and soon they cleared the forest and the Well of Segais lay beyond. Nimue was nowhere in sight. She approached scanning the distant treeline, but nothing, no one showed themselves. She sighed and sat next to the Wolf, pulling her knees up to her chin. She knew that to wait was wasting time, but through her short acquaintance with the pantheon, she also knew that they wouldn't hurry on anyone's account. Even Nimue, with Alexander, her son taken, wouldn't be moved to act before she was ready. Brenawyn was stuck here. She didn't know how to get home, to cross the veil, to find Maggie, to interact with anything here except ...

She looked at the Wolf, his eyes an iridescent amber, and she looked at the Well. The Wolf padded over to it and stepped in, wetting his front paws. He looked back at her and then to the depths.

"Well, all right, then," looking around to see if Nimue, Finvarra, or any other god appeared. "I don't think I should be doing this, but ... " She dove into the center of the Well. "No one is here to stop me." She took a deep breath and drove to the very bottom, the deepest part, choosing a hazelnut that lay in the silt of the sandy bottom; she had to dig through inches of nuts to get it.

By the time she chose, she felt the pressure of the lack of oxygen. Putting the nut, shell and all, in her mouth, she began battling back up to the surface. She burst through gasping for breath and the Wolf was there, paddling beside her. She took a fistful of his ruff and let him tow her back to the shore. Once there she climbed up and collapsed in the thick reeds just beyond the water line.

She took the nut out of her mouth, making it easier for her to breath, but the Wolf was there immediately nosing it in her hand. She turned over looking at the purplish sky and cracked the softened shell in her hands. Bracing for the pain she knew was coming, she squinted her eyes to shut out any light and put the nut in her mouth. Flavor, much like the coffee she so loved, exploded in her mouth from the softened meat. She slowly chewed, making sure to grind up the meat entirely before swallowing. She sucked on her teeth to get the tidbits that wedged in her molars. That gone she braved peeking out through an eye. The sky retained its purplish hue and she could see the Wolf pacing from the corner of her partially opened eye. She sat up slowly. Nothing changed. No pain. No vomiting. Nothing.

She wiped her hands on her wet jeans to rid them of pieces of nutshell and looked around confused. Was this the wrong well? She looked at the Wolf. "Well, it's not like I can ask you, insightful as you may seem." She was contemplating getting another as she squatted over the edge of the pool. As her hand broke the surface of the water, the reflection of the sky shifted and became cloudy, murky. She saw a cave lit by a sole lantern glinting off the slick reflective surfaces of stalagmites and the dark waters of an underground lake. A lantern sat on an unmanned boat, a lonely sentinel. She leaned in, the ends of her hair flopped in the reflection, scaring her, that the reflection would be gone, but no …

The boat was much closer now; it had but a single oar stuck in the oar lock. In the bottom arranged in perfect symmetry, were five white beeswax candles. She didn't need to see them to know that her stones: amethyst, tourmaline, obsidian, bloodstone, and tiger's eye were there also, a vision of the path she must travel, the conduit, not far.

The Wolf bolted to the safety of the trees when a voice boomed out behind them, "Interesting, I wonder what else she can dae?"

Brenawyn pivoted to see Nimue standing a short distance off with Finvarra. Standing next to each other, she noted similarities: ethereal, golden beauty, fair-hair, wide shoulders, his masculine, a sculpted chest and abdomen, hers willowy and feminine. But there was a familiar echo to their structure.

Brenawyn looked back at the reflection, gone now. Shit, what if it had something further to tell her: where, when, anything. She stirred the water, attempting to recreate the initial vision but nothing happened. It was done.

She got up to face Nimue and the other, still conversing quietly. She called out but they ignored her; she stepped closer, ignored again. She was losing patience and who knew how much time. She strode over to them and reached out to touch Nimue.

Finvarra, enraged, turned on her backing her up until she hit one of the hazelnut trees. "I ha' a mind ta test yer mettle again."

"Yeah well, wake me when it's over."

"Ye must learn how ta harness the power without expending yer own energy."

"Really?" Brenawyn responded sarcastically. "Since we're being obvious, might I add that of my two possible teachers, the first was dragged off by one of you for entertainment value and the other … that son of a bitch tied up."

"Are all mortals this irreverent or is it just you?"

"All mortals, especially ones," pointing at herself, "who don't give a damn."

"Remember the prophecy," said Finvarra. "The knowledge combined with an unknown ability from another line—together, she is the unknown quality, either our salvation or … "

"Or what?" Brenawyn piped up despite the nearness of Finvarra and his terrifying rage.

Nimue looked at her, silencing her companion. "Brenawyn, ye are either our salvation or our extinction. Choose wisely, though either choice willna bode well for ye. Yer fate, and hence ours, irrevocably tied together, is clouded. What is destined for us rests in the decisions ye make."

"Ye are giving her too much leverage. She kens nothing; else she wouldna ha' freely given her hand *and* her name. And ye trust her with the knowledge that she could bring about our ruin. Nimue, let me … "

Brenawyn sensed the brightness before she opened her eyes, the harsh jarring colors and vivid white light intruded casting a red haze over her lidded vision. She wished she could wait and adjust to the brutal change in light naturally, but need compelled her to move. Once she lifted her arm to brush away the grass seed heads tickling her cheeks, she realized she was stretched out with her hands at her sides, a totally unnatural way to fall, arranged this way probably by her grandmother—always trying to make people comfortable. Squinting, she located Leo a short distance away, sitting with her dog.

Brenawyn brought her hand up to shield her eyes, "How long was I out?"

"Long enough, but we're close, just over the next rise." She trailed off looking down at her empty hands, "What's it like, Brenawyn? Tir- Na-Nog?"

"It's beautiful. Like here but more."

"It is not for your ears, mortal." Brenawyn recoiled from the sound of Finvarra's voice, skittering away, retreating to a safer place; she turned in time to see him step out from tree hollow she was sat beside. Her grandmother fell to her knees, sobbing, at her side knowing that now after so many years she was going to face the wrath of the gods in performing the Phoenix. Even though it was used to save Brenawyn, it was not the enchantment's purpose. It was sacrilege to perform it for any other reason than the perpetuation of belief and history. She always knew that she'd have to face a reckoning. And it was pride that bolstered her naiveté over the twenty-nine years since her decision to employ it. After all, pride doeth cometh before the fall. She knew that time meant nothing to the gods. Her desperation wouldn't be accounted for, it would measure as an meager excuse. The gods did not love, not in the same way people did. Not for individuals. For children. Grandchildren.

Brenawyn bent to help her stand, but she batted her hands away, choosing to remain prostrate on the ground.

"Ye, Leoncha Anne Callahan are relieved o' yer responsibilities. Leave haur now or suffer my wrath."

Leo trembled on the ground, cowering lower. Finvarra rushed at Leo and grabbed her hair which had fallen loose from the ever present bun—fear etched every line, every winkle, accentuated the paleness of her strained face.

"Insolent mortal. For that alone, I should let Nimue ha' ye."

Brenawyn's heart hammered in her chest as she put her hand on his shoulder, "That won't be necessary." She expected an immediate rebuff, but instead felt the hardened muscles relax. Gaining some confidence from his reaction, she pulled his shoulder away. Power surged through his muscles under her fingers again, this time focused on her. If only he would let her grandmother go before he brought his wrath on Brenawyn. She couldn't have her be witness to it.

She placed her hand gently on his chest, a pitiful barrier to the building force behind it, and turned to her grandmother. "Go, Nana.

Clutching at her hand, Leo begged, "Brenawyn, no. I won't leave you."

Brenawyn squeezed her hand in reassurance and stepped back, her heart echoing what she felt in her now empty hand, "You have no choice. Neither of us do." Fear speared and she grasped her grandmother by the shoulders and embraced her. Would she ever see her again? "If I don't get back ... " She shook her gently, "Leo, listen to me. The paperwork for the car and bank accounts are in the boxes nearest the bed. You have access to the accounts and if you need more, sell the car." She pulled her grandmother to her chest. She could feel the frailty of her bones. When had she grown so thin? "Nana, I love you."

"There are so many things I wish to tell you. Here, put this on." Brenawyn looked down and saw the medallion she had left in her bedroom, "Never take it off."

She pressed her grandmother in the direction of relative safety. "You have to go now before he changes his mind."

But Leo pulled out the neck of Brenawyn's shirt and dropped the medallion in. "Remember, never take it off. Promise me," holding her hand over the fabric covered medallion.

Brenawyn pulled her to her feet. "I promise. Now, get out of here."

CHAPTER 13

Finvarra rose and slung his bow over his shoulder, "Come, we must go." He walked to Brenawyn and held out a hand. "I'm ta deliver ye ta yer instructor. T'is a long way even for sifting time."

Brenawyn slunk down to sit on the ground, the rough boulder at her back. It didn't even register that her shirt rode up in the back and she got scraped from her efforts. The only thing that mattered was obstinacy.

Finvarra looked amused, not the response she wanted. He chuckled, picked her up and threw her over his shoulder, "I like ye, Brenawyn McAllister for yer impertinence." He patted her rump. "But doona be deluded inta thinking ye ha' any control."

She screamed all combinations of expletives as she pummeled his back but he neither noticed nor cared.

Her surroundings, as much as she could see with her

hair over her face, were blurred but she had the impression of moving quickly between realms. Brief glimpses of the incandescent light and shimmering dryads of Tir-Na-Nog and the vibrant bright green world of her own flashed by. Somewhere along the way she gave up fighting and hugged his midsection so her head didn't bounce so much.

Holding her head that way strained her muscles so when he finally stopped and bent to take her off his shoulder, she cried out, clutching her midsection. She batted his hands away, turning her body to curl inward, to ease the screaming of her abdominal muscles. She shifted back but he was persistent. He gripped her thighs and yanked, her weight offering little resistance and he straddled her hips. Her body went rigid and bucked to get him off of her. Capturing both her wrists he held them above her head, "Hush, priestess, I am trying ta aid ye."

"Bullshit, you're trying to help yourself," she spat.

"Believe me, priestess," shook his head and Alexander's eyes looked into hers. "I ha' ne'er had ta resort ta force ... especially when I ha' other means o' persuasion at my fingertips."

She went still. Alexander—his eyes, his face, it couldn't be! If Brenawyn didn't see it herself, she wouldn't believe it.

"Dae ye ken that Alex was the only one who can shift? Who dae ye ken taught him ta dae that trick? Though he's no' gifted with the ability ta shift inta other than animals." He ground his hips down into hers. "Interested? No, I didna kin so." He placed his hand on her abdomen, lifting the shirt as he did, she started at the intimacy but he hushed her again, forcing her to lie flat. His hands were too warm and she had the conflicting urge to lean into them, press up against them, pleading for some of the warmth pooling in her belly to seep into her extremities. "If ye e'er ha' the penchant for a tryst," he leaned close, "call my name."

~~~

She awoke some time later shivering, hearing the echo of small movements and a distant drip, almost imperceptible. The darkness was consuming. She saw nothing, not even her hand in front of her face, as her eyes tried to adjust. Where was she? Her cheek was pressed against the damp smooth surface of a clay brick walkway, the solidity of rock at her back. There was a metallic click off to her right and—light! She squinted, trying to clear the large black spots from her vision. Once her irises adjusted, she saw that the feeble light shed by the lone battery lantern barely illuminated the slick surfaces off the surrounding walls. A stray drip, liquid ice, found its way through the gap in the neckline of her shirt. She knew where she was without having to let her eyes adjust to the dim light, if they ever would. She had seen this place in her vision, in her childhood, and as recently as that afternoon. She was in the caverns.

Movement off to her right startled her, "Doona fear. Nothing haur will harm ye. When ye are ready, we will begin."

The cave was ever changing, evolving. A living thing, the rush of the water over the stones father back and the slight pull here at the beginning of the lake, making the pools deeper. A chill pricked her skin. The statement that nothing would hurt her here was a misnomer. As long as she didn't move she'd be okay. A slight misstep in a thousand different places on the tourist trail would have her fall to break a bone or worse. Even with the hand railings looked rickety and slick next to the solidity of the rock all around.

She edged closer feeling for solid surface with her feet and scooted closer on her bottom towards the light from the lone lantern. The light, a beacon of safety linking her to civilization, was weak, consumed just a few feet from the lamp by the encroaching ancient darkness of the cavern.

Brenawyn jerked her head trying to pinpoint Finvarra but his voice echoed off the walls. "Extinguish the lantern, priestess."

She moved to protect it, pulling it into her lap, both fists wrapped around the handle. "No, it's the only light."

"The light needs to be snuffed in order to move away from the illusion of safety and logic."

She huddled closer to it as if the small heat thrown off by the fluorescent light was enough to heat her chilled skin. "Safety, logic, and warmth are good. I'll stay here, thank you." She heard the sharp intake of breath probably through his nose, Liam used to do that, the first sign that he was losing patience.

"I am approaching ye on yer left. I would appreciate it if ye didna lash out." He placed a hand on her shoulder and sat next to her. It didn't seem like he was having trouble in the darkness but why would he? He was a god after all. "I am going ta hold yer hand until ye get comfortable. Is that acceptable?" His fingers closed over hers. "Well met." He squeezed her hand, "Tell me, Brenawyn McAllister, why did ye accept yer legacy?"

She turned to him, even this close, the dark made it almost impossible to make out the details of his countenance. "Well, um ... "

"I ken the reason, but ye need ta hear yerself say it."

"For Alex ... Alexander. I didn't, I don't want him to be hurt."

"So yer humanity made ye act the way ye did." He scoffed. "Try again."

She shied away but he tightened his grip on her hand, "Och nay, *priestess*, ye canna escape me. Ye will answer in the dark." He reached over and wrenched the lantern away. It crashed against the near wall, the light guttering. "Confession in the dark," he unclasped her hand, but remained next to her. "Convince yerself that t'is only ye ta hear."

Brenawyn remained silent, consumed with more than a childish fear of the dark; it was the instinctual dread of the unknown, of the complete blackness of the bowels of the Earth. She cringed toward him, a lesser evil, but he hardened, another rock formation carved out over millions of years. There was no succor there.

Why had she accepted the terms? It certainly wasn't because she was a believer. She may eventually be able to accept these others considering themselves to be deities but she knew her God. That didn't answer anything though; it didn't bring her closer to the truth. Perhaps she was looking at this wrong, perhaps she was making this too complicated.

Alexander. Why Alexander? She was drawn to him. She needed him. The runes. Accepting the fact that they were ... fact, they gave some credence to ... what? Didn't they? She felt they had a connection to her feelings but she couldn't put it to words.

Brenawyn opened her mouth, not in confession but for herself, "All my life I have felt like I didn't belong, like I was born at the wrong time. Things happened in my life: my mother's death, I was so young. I don't feel like I ever had a connection with her. My father, he put the distance there, holding me at arm's length. He made it so there wasn't a deep connection. Liam, that was all a lie. Then there is my grandmother, the only one I have a connection with. And somehow I think this," igniting her runes so they flared over her skin, "had something to do with that. Then came Alexander, and a deep connection that belies the short time we've known each other. I am compelled to go to him."

"I am reminded o' the children's toy that uses equal distribution o' weight.

She laughed surprised, "What are you talking about?

"Two children sitting on opposite ends teeter back and forth."

"Do you mean a see-saw? What reason do you have for considering a piece of playground equipment ... no, don't answer that, I don't want to know."

"The design is no' unlike the early conception o' the catapult; but I digress. Suppose one child was much heavier or on the other hand, non-existent. What would happen ta the game?"

"The game would have to be amended to take into account the unequal weight. It is all about balance and if there is only one child, there wouldn't be one at all."

"Hm. balance. The cosmos, fate, what ha' ye, has a way o' ensuring balance. The transmigration o' the soul is aberrant, in this case, and perhaps yer feeling is an integral part o' setting the balance ta rights."

"One person is not that important."

"To yer mere mind perhaps no'."

"Tell me about this balance."

"In order for me to do so I have to relay history."

Brenawyn settled against the rock as comfortably as she could, "From wherever you feel you should start."

"I am High King of the Tuatha Dé Danann."

"Hm, pleasant."

"I am as I was meant to be. I doona find it a hardship."

"Go on."

"I am part o' a small contingent who chose ta remain haur. As part o' the Accord drawn up after the third battle o' Magh Tuireadh whaur the Tuatha Dé were defeated by the Milesians. We have limited access … "

"Third battle?"

Finvarra heaved a sigh. "Let me begin at the beginning."

"Fantastic idea. Please do."

"The Tuatha Dé are descendants o' Nemed, a Formoir, who had already inhabited the land ye refer ta as Ireland. We didna refer ta ourselves as such yet, not until long after. Thaur was a war, in which only few survived. We had ta flee, the original group splintering and going different ways. I was with the group that headed north. We suffered devastating losses but our hearts were set on vengeance, but we were weak, and those who could fight scattered. We heard whispers o' cities that honed skills, and we set out ta find such teachers. Eventually we found them one by one, in the fabled cities o' Falias, Gorias, Murias, and Finias. We acquired skills and developed attributes in the art o' magic, learning glamours, manipulation o' the elements, sifting time, shape-shifting, and augury. Each city had its own specialty, and when we were ready ta move on, we were given a talisman from each."

"How long did this take?"

"Many millennia, but when our training was complete we were the Tuatha Dé Danann, ready ta go back ta reclaim our home and seek vengeance for our fallen."

"So you regrouped."

"Aye, and multiplied. So when we arrived on Conmaicne Rein, we brought a darkness that settled over the land for three days and nights."

"That ominous arrival probably did not endear you to the inhabitants."

Finvarra shrugged his shoulders, "What is no' kent is feared, what is feared must be destroyed. Is it no' this way with humans?"

Brenawyn laughed sardonically, "It seems that sentiment transcends time, place, race."

"And realms too. Although it couldna be helped, we

ultimately invaded, though we did try diplomacy first. Our terms were rejected as we kent from prophecy they would be, the first battle o' Magh Tuireadh was fought. The battle was fierce, our acquired skills only enabling a level playing field."

Finvarra moved the lantern closer. Brenawyn looked up and thought at first it was just the shadows changing on his face, but the longer she looked, the realization hit her that his face was changing. Bone structure and muscles moved beneath his skin. A white, puckered scar appeared bisecting his left eyebrow and ripping down his cheek. She moved closer, hand outstretched to touch his face.

"Careful, if ye willingly touch me, ye'll be mine."

Brenawyn paused in her movement as the changes continued. His long blonde hair was shortening to a severely cropped shock of red. "I'm sure I've touched you before in Tir-Na- ... fairyland."

"My gauntlet, yes, I can still feel yer warm touch, even though it was through metal. That one wouldna affect ye as this one would. Our skin emits a marker. If ye touch the Lord of the Tuatha Dé, mortal, yer skin against mine, I'll be able ta call ye whenever the whim strikes."

Brenawyn snatched her hand away, hugging it to her chest. "What the hell?"

"Are ye sure, priestess? I could awaken pleasures ye didna ken existed."

"No, thank you. I have no desire to be your thrall."

Finvarra bowed, "As ye wish." With a wave of his hand, he indicated his new appearance, "Nuada. Leader of the Tuatha Dé against the Fir Bolg."

175

Brenawyn resettled against the rock at her back. "Wait."

"Aye, priestess?"

"I did touch the goddess in the clearing. Caer Ibormeith, was that her name?"

Finvarra nodded, "And so ye did."

"Will she be able to call me?"

"Aye, she will, but doona worry, she rarely does. As a limitation ta her dominion, she relies on touch in order to See.

"So she won't call me to thralldom then?"

"A little late ta be concerned o'er much about the deal ye've made."

"I guess you're right. Go on then."

Finvarra stood and a sword appeared in his hand. He grabbed the longsword and raised the hilt to his temple, blade near horizontal pointing at a would-be opponent's throat. "The fighting was fierce, but it came down to each sides' champions, Nuada, and the Fir Bolg's Sreng."

Finvarra-Nuada moved gracefully, changing the position of the sword angled up to what appeared to be in the vicinity of the opponent's chest. His movements became quicker and more fluid. Brenawyn didn't know where to look in the light cast by the lantern. Finvarra danced throughout the cast light coming to a stop in front of Brenawyn, sword poised at forty-five degrees angled over his head, looking down at her, "But then," he whispered, "disaster."

He was rocked back by an unseen blow, severing his arm just below the shoulder, the sword clattering to her feet. She was too shocked to scream, but only had forethought to plaster herself to the rock wall behind her.

The severed arm vanished before it hit the ground, the spurting blood gone. Brenawyn shook her head, but soon realized it was all an illusion. Finvarra-Nuada stood in front of her sans his right arm smiling slightly and sighed. "Nuada won the day, but was no longer able to lead."

"He won the battle and was demoted?"

"Aye, that is the way o' the Tuatha Dé. The leader has ta be whole, and Nuada was no longer. He was given care though. Dian Cecht, a healer, was employed ta stanch the wound and build a prosthetic arm."

"Oh, huh. I thought they were a relatively modern invention."

"Nay. They are no'. The arm that Dian made was o' silver, but by the time the arm was finished, a replacement king was coronated. Bres, a half-Fomorian, assumed leadership.

Finvarra's bone structure moved again and the scar disappeared. The short, cropped red hair grew and darkened into a black mane past his shoulders. A heavy brow settled over eyes as black as midnight. He added another six or more inches to his already imposing height, packing on more muscle to his chest, arms, and legs. Finvarra-Bres looked down on Brenawyn. "But, Bres was a tyrant, imposing ridiculous laws and enslaving the Tuatha Dé."

Brenawyn nodded comprehension.

"Thaur were whispers o' rebellion, but nay plan until Dian Cecht's son and apprentice, Miach, without the knowledge o' his father, cast a spell ta ha' flesh grow over Nuada's silver armature. Appearing whole again, it didna take long for Nuada's resurrection ta spread, and without a single drop o' blood lost, deposed Bres, and was restored.

Bres didna take the loss so easily. He went immediately ta his father, Elatha, and was sent ta his grandfather, Balor, king o' the Fomorians. Nemed's truce between the Tuatha Dé Danann and the Formorians … "

"The same Nemed whose war had you flee to the North?"

"Aye, the same. The ancient truce was broken and thus the second battle o' Magh Tuireadh."

"Between the Formorians and the Tuatha Dé."

"Aye, but this time," Finvarra-Bres' bones moved again. The mane of dark hair became shaggier, and he shrank a bit, becoming broader in the shoulders and thicker in the belly. His face was grotesquely malformed to accommodate one larger eye socket. The sclera of this eye intruded on the iris clouding and covering it over until just the black pupil stood out in hideous contrast.

Brenawyn gasped.

"Balor's poisonous eye killed Nuada."

"Does that eye, and the Oracle's have anything in common?"

"Verra perceptive ye are, but that can wait."

"So, the Formorians won the second battle?"

"Nay, the Tuatha Dé did, but only because a new champion, Lugh, stepped up and killed Balor. Some claim it was luck that Lugh stayed out of Balor's gaze, but I was thaur. Lugh had the spear talisman crafted in Findias with him which ensured victory."

"So how many years between the second and third battle of … what did you call it?"

"Magh Tuireadh"

"Moy Tirra."

"Good. Ye ha' an ear for languages."

"Thank you."

"Many of yer lifetimes between the two, so many, in fact, that Lugh died, and the spear talisman was lost."

"That's unlucky for your people."

"Quite. The Accord struck after the third battle represents the balance."

Brenawyn laughed, "And you want me to do what exactly? Be a warrior, some kind of champion? Good luck. I'd just as likely sever a limb. I know nothing of strategy nor have the physical stamina that it would take." Brenawyn stopped and sobered. "No, that's not what you need me to do, is it? A diplomat? A politician to head some kind of interdimensional summit?"

"Doona be flippant."

"I am not who you think I am. I can't stop a war."

"Regardless of yer feelings, ye ha' been recognized by the gods as the priestess. Ye are who we've been waiting for. Ye must do yer duty."

"And what is that exactly?"

"You are descended from the Milesians, to whom the Tuatha lost the last battle. Your ancestors wrote the Accords that allowed a contingent of the Tuatha De to remain in Tir-Na-Nog."

"Why would they do that?"

"We had something they wanted."

Brenawyn thought for a moment, "Ah, magic!"

"Aye. Magic. Negotiations lasted almost a lifetime."

"Neither side wanted to yield."

Finvarra bowed his head, "But I am patient, and Tanaris, the God of Death more so, many who come ta stand in front of him try ta negotiate a longer life bartering things in their minds were theirs to give, but in fact, they ne'er possessed. T'is only a matter o' time 'afore they wear themselves out, and come ta accept the inevitable."

"And was it the same negotiating this contract?"

"Alas, nay, t'was no'."

"What was different?"

Finvarra looked at her askance, and smirked. "I always get what I want."

"That had to burn then?"

His brows rose, "Priestess, do ye think this was not exactly what I wanted?"

It was Brenawyn's turn to be surprised. "Okay. So why would you want to have the bulk of your people exiled?"

"Ask yerself, why."

"Had to be something in it for you. Power?"

He bowed his head again. "Why?"

"To claim devotion and perhaps fear."

"Many o' the Tuatha De didna kin the Milesians worthy o' our magic."

"So none of them are still around."

Finvarra laughed, a melodious baritone. "Nay. They

are no'."

"So you're an opportunist, but it still doesn't explain why it has to be me."

"Ye are the only daughter of an only daughter, going back through the ages ta a time before the Accords."

"That can still be coincidence."

"But in the time before the first were exiled, Formorian blood was intermixed with yer own. Then Tuatha Dé blood was introduced. Finally, the last was added."

"Milesian."

"Aye. Ye are the Accords."

CHAPTER 14

"Dae ye believe Maggie was taken from ye?"

"Yes, you and my grandmother give the same account. So I believe it."

"A'richt, dae ye believe Alexander was taken from ye?"

"Yes, because I saw it with my own eyes."

"Dae ye believe that he is being held until Samhain?"

"That was outlined in the verbal agreement. So, yes, I have to believe it, don't I?"

"No, ye doona, but let's put that aside for now and proceed on the premise that everything that ye ha' been told is true. On the belief that Alexander is imprisoned, ye ha' accepted the role prophesied and ha' agreed to the terms of Cernunnos."

"I suppose I have."

"In order to do that, I must aid ye in performing the

Rite o' Widdershins. This incantation will take ye bodily back ta a time when thaur is a need. Usually t'is done in service o' some wrong that needs ta be righted. In yer case, ye need ta find a mentor, since the one at hand is now unavailable. Ye will be unprepared and thus, at a great disadvantage. I kin no' which era ye must return ta, ta seek the answers. The information ye need is beyond me, beyond any o' the other gods. Ye canna travel the way we do, and thaur was ne'er a need for us ta travel any other way. The only way ye will find yer path is ta offer ta make yerself apprentice ta the Merlin."

"Apprentice to Merlin? As in the legendary Merlin? King Arthur and Camelot.?"

"Doona believe the stories that ha' been presented ta ye. The Merlin is a title for the Shaman o' the Order. Ye are in search o' the Merlin Who Was. Everything is in readiness but for the memory o' the ritual. "Will ye allow me?"

Brenawyn felt herself nod. In for a penny, in for a pound. Her priorities were adjusting; she wasn't sure if it was a good thing. "What do I need to do?"

Finvarra clasped her face between his two large hands, the movement startling in the dark. "Relax, this is no' going ta hurt." He leaned in, "Count ta three and inhale sharply."

One, two, three. She smelled wildflowers and freshly turned soil—the dark of night, a bonfire, a straight backed old man chanting over five candles, a young man prostrate on the ground, only visible from the glowing runes. A shift in position, the old man sagged, his runes dulled, helped

183

by the other, whose sigils turned painfully bright.

Brenawyn felt Finvarra sit back but he still held her face though softly now.

"The Rite o' the Phoenix properly done. Now for Widdershins."

He leaned in again. "The same as before, priestess."

She inhaled the cloying aroma of wilted roses, the edges of the petals dry and curling, the smell intense but with an underlying hint of decay assailed her sensed as her mind's eye saw a lone woman kneeling in the midst of pillars of flame. The words she uttered incomprehensible, but the thought compelled Brenawyn to focus on them. A word became understandable, then another, three, more. The she was gone. The flames burned low in her absence.

"This is the basis for what ye need." He held her face for a long second. "Come. All is in readiness. I will help ye into the boat."

Brenawyn followed close enough to feel his subtle body movements. She stopped when he did and grasped the slick metal handrail when guided. The squeak of the gunwale on the foam rubber padding along the dock gave her a direction to face even though her eyes would not adjust to the darkness. The weight of vulnerability was easier to bear if she faced the general direction.

"Haur," Finvarra took her hand. Step forward. Dae ye feel the edge?"

Before she could answer, she was swept off her feet and deposited on the vinyl seat bench. "What's next?"

"Ye travel alone from haur."

"What do you mean alone?"

"I must leave ye haur. It must be this way."

"But what if I am not who you hope I am."

"Ye are the priestess, ye ha' taken the mantle voluntarily. The only point o' contention remaining is if ye are the prophesied priestess. Everything ye do from point o' agreement must be done through yer own volition."

"But how do I ... "

"Thaur are things ye must ken. I canna tell ye the time or place ta which ye travel."

"Do you mean I won't even be in the same place?"

"Widdershins balances the universe by returning order. Whaure'er, whene'er the rift first began, the traveler goes ta correct and heal."

"So, I will be alone? Don't answer that. I have a feeling it won't sound any better hearing it. Can I ask a question?"

"Certainly, priestess."

"Why didn't Cernunnos take me when he had the chance? He knew who I was the moment I touched him."

"He is the King o' the Wild Hunt with prey in sight. He is a slave ta his own instincts and that took precedent. The lure o' free will is lost on humans. Ye doona see what an incredible ability it is ta choose. Once the agreement was made, ye bound yerself ta him for all eternity or at least until the independent spirit finally dies in ye. He will be a harsh taskmaster, pitting ye against more difficult tasks designed ta make ye choose. The three months until Samhain is a single heartbeat. He is waiting in anticipation for yer arrival."

"This will not interfere with the duties of the high priestess?"

"Ye have little knowledge o' the affairs o' the gods. T'will no' interfere, in fact, for the Order, t'is a good thing that ye are in service ta Cernunnos. Yer life will be extended much, much longer than what it would be. As a mere woman, in good health, ye would live eighty, ninety years, as priestess four times as long, and in servitude ta a god, nigh immortal, if ye are clever enough ta keep his interest."

"Will my presence draw attention from Alexander?"

"Aye, though I canna estimate yer worth in diversion, though if it were me ye promised yerself I could think o' many ways ye could entertain. Are ye sure I canna entice ye? My will supersedes his own."

"No, thank you. I have enough on my plate now."

"Up haur, next ta me is a bag of ritual supplies ta set up whaur ye will along the way. After the incantation, all will seem ta remain the same until ye depart the cave. Behind ye, I ha' provided better clothes ta traverse the rock and various small tools ye will need ta do so. Ye must ha' the rucksack on yer person 'afore starting the incantation or risk leaving it behind."

"Give me the lantern then."

Finvarra handed it to her in the dark, "Ye willna need it."

"You are not confident about the destination. What happens if the walkways are gone and I have to spelunk? A thought that obviously entered your thinking else the backpack stuffed with cave exploration supplies wouldn't exist. I will be caught down here, far from the surface, with no light, no life down here, except perhaps a bat colony, before the disease hit that killed them off in this time. Of course there is the moss, but that can't be counted because its existence is only possible through manmade interference of electricity."

"If having the lantern makes ye feel more confident, take it." He rose, the boat moving at the change in the dispersement of weight. "If thaur is nothing else, I will help ye ta the back o' the boat. The pole awaits."

He picked her up again to deposit her on the short platform at the stern and handled a pole to her. "I will light the lantern for ye ta ease yer way."

Brenawyn could now see his face illuminated by the weak battery light of the camp lantern, but it did little else to light her way down the Lake of Venus.

He shifted and was gone. "Wait," she called out, and he was back whispering in her ear though she didn't feel the boat shift this time. "Haur, open yer hand."

"What is it?"

"Pulverized rock from the stream bed beyond. Repeat after me and blow on the dust. *Taispeáin an solas dom*. It means, 'show me the light.'"

Brenawyn nodded and translating the words in her head to speak aloud and blew on the handful of dust in her hand. The dust hung in the air swirling on an unfelt breeze and then ignited expanding to the roof of the cavern and spreading down the twisting length of the waterway. Brenawyn looked up in wonder at the night sky with tiny twinkling pinpricks.

"Haur. Keep this in yer pocket."

She shoved the sand into her pocket careful not to drop any. A most useful trick. She'd certainly use it.

"Ye must go. Doona use the remainder haur. Save it until ye get ta yer destination. Ye can call the light." With a whisper of a caress on her cheek, he was gone, and she had the arduous task of poling her way to the dam. She didn't need to spend any time deliberating the location she needed when she remembered always daydreaming about the spot when she was younger. The tour guides never could tell her. Logic dictated that they didn't know themselves, but alone in the womb of the Earth perhaps they didn't want to name their fear or scare people. What was beyond the drop?

Brenawyn's muscles ached by the time she could see the double chains glinting off the magic illumination. She tested the depth, two feet perhaps, and steered to the last alcove, slamming the bow against the rock scraping the length of the boat to slow its forward momentum. She lost her balance with the initial jarring but recovered in time to save herself from a dunk in the cold water before she was ready.

Scampering over the benches, she collected the materials for the ritual and hooked the backpack onto a shoulder. Testing one last time, she decided to bring the pole to test the waters further up and to use as a walking stick, awkward but for the length. She had no illusions for a smooth surface on the lake bottom.

She sat on the gunwale making the large boat canter to the side at an alarming angle. Not good. She had no choice but to reevaluate, taking the backpack off her shoulder to place it where she could reach it on the bottom of the boat with the candles and stones. She used the pole to judge the depth again, estimating a large flat rock. Saying a quick prayer that she didn't strain an ankle she vaulted into the water. She wasn't prepared for the icy temperature, never gave it a thought before, but with a constant temperature of near fifty degrees raising gooseflesh on her naked arms in the cave, its water left her breathless and shivering. It took endless seconds for her to regain motor control and gather the items she stored. Trudging through the water, the rocky

outcropping mere inches above the waterline looked like heaven.

She pushed the bags on top the shelf sure to keep them away from the edge and the encroaching darkness beyond. She hoisted herself up, ripping at the zipper, eager to peel the wet jeans away from her chilled skin. She rummaged through the backpack and found serviceable overalls, pilfered from the gatehouse from the looks of them. She didn't care, they were dry and warm, pooling at her ankles and covering her fingers. She'd roll them up in a bit once her teeth stopped chattering.

Brenawyn looked back along the waterway. Was the light becoming dimmer? Shit. Where was it? Did the pocket get wet? She didn't want to contemplate the effect of water on the dust. There, oh thank God, it was still dry. She poured it out carefully into the oversized pockets of the overalls, turning the pocket inside out to try to get the remainder. She'd have to remember to conserve the remainder, perhaps she could use a portion of it at a time, rationing it out. It would take her considerably longer to exit the cave. Shit. Could she find more? Would it work?

Calm down. What was the use of panicking now?

Brenawyn pulled the other bag toward her, extracting the five new candles and stones, the same kind as before, just highly polished and faceted. She arranged them around her, holding the fifth candle for spirit with the bloodstone wedged between her knees as she knelt on the rocky edge.

Once done, she took inventory of the backpack, a nylon tarp, glow sticks, matches in a sealed plastic container, before jamming her wet jeans into the bag, rolling them in the tarp, unwilling to leave anything behind. She flipped the pack over her head slipping her arms through the loops and attached the lantern with the thin bungee cords that laced the front of it.

With a deep breath bringing the image Finvarra placed in her mind of the lone woman she began.

> *In the name of all the spirits both shade and light*
> *Grant me sight so I may know truth*
> *To piece together purpose in prophecy*
> *Lost and blind, knowing not how to restore balance*
> *But recognized by fate and acknowledged to fulfill the*
> *   will*
> *Guidance by Surcellos I beg ...*

CHAPTER 15

Finvarra glamoured through the wall that held Alex prisoner. "She has undergone Widdershins."

Alex pivoted to face Finvarra, "By herself? Whaur is she? How dae ye ken this?"

"Part of her bargain with my consort and that of your jailor, her father."

"Did ye guide her? Ye ne'er dae anything ye are asked without yer own compensation."

"She was very single-minded, nothing would ha' distracted her; she is the most intriguing human I ha' met. Comparable ta ye, in fact. I am looking forward ta when we meet again, but until she calls my name, I ha' ta wait." He approached and clapped him on the shoulder. "The end is near, either for good or ill. She will be our salvation or our destruction. Ha' faith."

"Aye, Finvarra, I dae ha' faith, but thaur is no hope

for me, the Wild Hunt is elemental."

"Alexander Morgan Sinclair, all hope is not lost for whene'er she is, she is no' alone. She carries yer progeny."

A burning desire welled from the pit of his stomach. A desire so elemental, to find Brenawyn and cocoon her against all harm. He couldn't do anything here, in this place, this glass prison, but out there. Yea, that was where he needed to be. He needed to exert his frustration and nothing spoke to that need like the Hunt. The sluaghs would bring him to ground; he'd welcome it this time, relish the pain, for through the pain came resurrection and heightened ability. If he could manage to run the course a couple of times, it had never been asked before by prey to willingly go into the Stalking Grounds, but he didn't see a reason for the request to be denied. All he'd have to do was anger the god again. That would be easy. Such rage and frustration, held back after centuries of servitude. No, it wouldn't be hard to anger the god. He wished he was a better judge on how time passed between the two realms to judge how long he had, how many times he could run the course. He'd have to get out before Samhain, so he'd be free to protect her from Cormac and the rest of the Coven. He turned to Finvarra, decision made, "Call Cernunnos. I want ta renegotiate."

He couldn't tell the passage of time from the light outside the window. Above the trees it was the same light as in Tir-Na-Nog, indirect and bright, but below it barely traversed the thick canopy. What little that did make it through was further swallowed by the thick sheets of moss hanging from the branches. Small ripples from questing fish broke the stagnant stillness of the water but even that was suddenly quiet as a more menacing shadow undulated just under the surface. If only there were more light, Alex would be able to see what it was that lurked there. Another predator, one he hadn't come in contact with yet. Perhaps it would be its turn this time when he went in.

He paced the length of windows, falling into routine as so many times before. Was it his imagination that saw a wear mark along this path? He's certainly paced it enough over the centuries.

Alex knew he wasn't alone and turned, surprised to find Cernunnos standing there. He had to bend to fit inside the room, and even so then his antlers scraped against the ceiling, shaving off plaster so it fell like snow on his shoulders. "

"I was told ye want ta renegotiate. Ta go into the arena now. Is this true, Shaman?"

"Ye ha' heard correctly."

"Yer request is denied, superseded by another."

"Ye ha' no' heard my reasoning."

"It matters not; she has made herself kent ta me. Ye will bide until such time as she comes ta take yer place."

"Take my place? How could ye dae that ta yer daughter who has been lost ta ye for nigh on five hundred and seventy years?"

"I ha' a task for her. T'is none o' yer concern, in fact, yer services are no longer required. An apprentice has been chosen and when it comes time, ye will transfer yer abilities o' yer office. Ye will retain what ye ha' gained from the resurrections, then all that remains will be the demands o' the Wild Hunt."

"I doona ha' any illusions as ta my fate, it will be haur or thaur until the end o' time, but t'is my obligation ta choose the next Merlin."

"The responsibility has been taken from ye by the elders. "They feel ye ha' lost yer objectivity. They ha' chosen Cormac Domhaill MacBrehon."

"Never."

"T'is beyond yer control."

"Never. MacBrehon was discarded as a choice the last time. Six hundred years have not mellowed him. He is arrogant and cruel, corrupted by power and eager for the kill. He murdered Colleen, after she … " a cry ripped from his throat and he turned his back on the god. "She was my woman, I had nay claim ta her, but I loved her nonetheless. Meeting clandestinely for stolen moments during the Choosing. I couldna help myself; she was so … gods, she was beautiful and innocent.

After I was chosen, he got to her, played on her insecurities. I would have found a way to be with her, but I was called away so often in the beginning and he was thaur, freed from the selection process. He listened ta her frustrations about the separation. I doona ken when he started ta court her; I wasn't privy ta that part. Just forced ta watch, as part o' my torture haur. Ye should ken that, ye ordered it ta break me."

"She was not worthy of you."

"I'll never know."

"Can a human change so much?"

"Depends on the circumstances for each person I

194

think. Some will never change, like Cormac, except to slide more into darkness. Mark my words, he is a heretic."

CHAPTER 16

How long was Brenawyn supposed to wait here for something to happen before she gathered her nerve and found her way out of here? It would be easier once she poled her way back to the dock, but she had just the lantern, unless the electricity worked from the switch on the wall somewhere to her left.

She let the pack slide down her arms and reached for the lantern getting to her feet before lighting it. The battery powered light glowed yellow illuminating the *empty* platform. No candles, no stones, no push button for the electricity anchored to the limestone on the left wall.

Panic set in. The lantern thumped on the stone, cantered and spun teetering on the edge for a second before falling. In slow motion, she lunged for it but it was too late, the lantern landed six feet below, still lit, in the pool of the stream bed. She skittered back from the edge and crouched with her head in her hands.

Breathe.

This is what you expected to happen—pull yourself together, get the gear together, go for the lamp, there is an exit this way too.

Brenawyn flung the pack onto her back tying the straps around her waist for extra security. She scooted to the edge and rolled so her belly was flat on the precipice, her legs dangling off. She tore at her nails, ripping off the edges so they wouldn't be in the way as she gripped the finger holds she found in the limestone. Inch by inch, she climbed down, unsure of the footholds she found, tensing on each, until she knew they could hold her weight. It was tough going, the rock slick with moisture, but she touched down on the rocky stream bed next to the natural pool and collapsed to sit. She hooked the lantern's handle with the edge of her boot and hauled it to her, shaking off the water. The lantern still glowed as bright, but here in the deep recesses it didn't illuminate as far. What was she to do if the light gave out? Then she remembered. Did Finvarra's gift make it with her?

She reached into the deep pocket to find the dust. Oh thank God! She took a handful out, careful not to drop any. What was the phrase? *Taispeáin an solas dom* and blew on the dust. The sand ignited and spread through the air, moving at an alarming speed, then flew up and raced against the ceiling, casting light on all below. Brenawyn switched off the lantern to save battery power.

She walked picked her way carefully on the slippery rocks, heading deeper into the earth. She blew on more dust periodically, muttering the same phrase, rewarded with light to further her journey. She hiked through the rocks, scrambling over stalagmites that fell eons ago, Following the twinkling lights, she came to a dead end and looked up to the spiraling lights as they twisted up. Brenawyn put her pack down, knowing what she needed to do if ever she was going to be free. She thought of going back but the steep climb was more than she could bear. She tried the dust anyway, but the lights only went up. She'd be lost forever in these caves if she went back down. She no longer had the man-made trails to judge her whereabouts.

The shaft was tight, little more than a body's width, and if that were the case, she'd be able to use pressure to keep from falling. There was a coil of nylon rope in the pack, along with a grappling hook and carabiners. She went slowly, wedging her back against the wall before venturing up, more concerned with finding a secure foothold than what was keeping her from falling to her death, broken on the slabs below. The space became tighter as she put her hands on rock covered in light dust that glinted and faded out as she passed. At least she couldn't frighten herself by looking down. Her fingers and toes ached from gripping. The muscles in her legs and arms screamed. The space was getting smaller, closing in on her. This was no time for claustrophobia. She came to the end of the line, where the reminder of the light clustered in front of her. Now what? She couldn't go down.

She maneuvered and the hook scraped on the wall.

She gripped the handle and took a half swing that was all the space would allow at the point. The rock gave easily, crumbling away, showering her with chunks of limestone. She gave another series of whacks; more chunks fell away. She could feel a breeze and it gave her strength to keep hacking.

It was a long time before she had an opening large enough to pull herself through but when she did, she had no interest in looking to see where she ended up. Somewhere in the vicinity of the caverns, but it was dark, night, and she was so tired. Crawling away from the opening she curled up in a depression behind a fallen log, pillowing her head on her pack before dropping off to sleep.

She came awake in increments, listening to the sounds of the birds and small animals scurry around her. Soon enough she'd have to deal with where she was, but she would keep her eyes closed for just a few more minutes.

What was that?

Brenawyn heard voices whispering. They had seen her. Shit. Time to deal. She opened her eyes and at first didn't see anyone. "Hello?"

"Och, she's awake. The sleeping lady's awake. Da's got ta be told." A rustle of leaves and brush, identified the retreating forms of two gawky boys in kilts. "Bide," the taller told his brother, "we canna lose her." The younger looked back at Brenawyn, conflicting emotions racing across his face. He obviously wanted to stay to claim whatever bragging rights there were to be had, but he was skeptical, looking at her as if she were a snake. She stood up and took a step towards him, and he shied away. Perhaps she'd be able to get a location from the father when he arrived.

She judged the boy was no danger and sat down on the log. She was in a ravine; a stone bridge spanned the gap above her. She was no expert, and certainly never looked at the structural quality of anything, but didn't concrete and steel buttresses need to be there for support?

"What's your name?" she called.

His mouth gaped as he turned his head in the direction of his now absent brother and took a few steps back.

"I won't hurt you." She tried to allay his fears, still sitting on the log. "I'm lost. Could you tell me where I am?"

Again, nothing. She gave up. If he wasn't going to answer her she'd better find someone who would. Perhaps if she went in the direction of the brother she'd run into someone who could give her information. But in the time it took her to swing the pack on her back, she heard a group approach.

"Och laddie, it be too many o' the auld stories ye be hearin' around the fire. Be speakin' ta yer da tonight, I will."

"I doona need ta confess. Ye'll see."

The two came around the bend and the woman stopped midstride so the brother walked into her rocking her forward on her feet.

Brenawyn stood up brushing at the wrinkles in her overalls, as if that would help. The woman was petite, with a kerchief holding back her long greying hair. The first real indication that she was in the past was the woman's dress. She wore a rough woven blouse and skirt under a long apron. She had a cape wrapped around her to guard her against the cold.

"Och, St. Bride save us. T'is the sleeping lady." She was shaking visibly, "Laddie, go find yer da. Bring him back ta the keep. Go, take yer brother too."

"Hi, um, I'm Brenawyn McAllister. Could you tell … "

"No' the now. Come, ye canna be seen as ye are. T'is indecent." Rushing to her side, she twirled the cape off her shoulders and onto Brenawyn's, in one fluid movement, effectively hiding her coveralls. "Come, I'll slip ye inta the keep, find ye something suitable ta wear, and then ye'll get yer questions answered.

"But, if you would just..."

"I doona mean ta be discourteous," she said, looking around at the surrounding shrubbery with suspicion, pinning the ends of the cloth with a silver broach, "but thaur are people who would be frightened and it wouldna bode well for ye."

Brenawyn had no choice but to trail after her. She was in a different time, and she could have appeared in much less desirable circumstances. She'd follow this woman for the time being, allow her to find appropriate clothing that would help her fit in better, until at least, she opened her mouth and announced that she was from some other place. She was obviously in Scotland or Ireland. She'd never paid any mind to the different dialects, and didn't know if the distinction would help her now. What could she say about her own place of origin? A woman, her speech and her pronunciations markedly different, traveling alone? Could she ask to see the Merlin? Should she make reference to the Druids? Her first instinct was to reveal nothing until she had a better bead on where and when she was.

The grade of the land became steep, calling for all of her focus to not trip over the folds of the cloak. The woman, who was not even short of breath from the climb, had to turn and wait for her frequently.

"Och, gi' me the bag. With all yer huffing, ye'll sure attract the whole clan's attention."

Without the bag, it was easier, because it wasn't pulling her off balance. They gained the edge and Brenawyn held her side, breathing deeply through her mouth, but the woman marched on, figuring Brenawyn to follow now that the ground was even.

She stood at the edge of a stone bridge, the same that spanned the ravine, with guard towers on either side. She saw movement in the shadows of the thin openings, eyes staring down at her. The woman hurried back, took her arm and led her on, beyond the sight of the tower. "I should ha' waited 'til the dark ta bring ye. When we get ta the end o' the path, hurry, like yer busy at yer tasks, and for all that is holy, keep yer head doon. Follow me but not as close as we would be seen walking together. Ye ken, aye?"

"Yes. I can do that. What is your name?"

"Later, lassie. Later."

They passed through the matching towers, unmanned, and into an open courtyard. Brenawyn passed small structures easily identifiable as stables, smokehouse and a blacksmith's forge were closest to the gate and furthest away from the main dwelling for ease and probably safety from fire. They passed a large draft horse pulling a cart full of peat as they reached the kitchen. This was attached to the main keep, the largest building and, it turned out, this was where they were heading.

Without looking back, the woman entered the kitchens. As she entered silence fell as the roomful of women stopped amid their duties, one with her hands still in the dough she was kneading, another taking bread out of the wood oven. A loaf fell in the cinders, showering the skirt of a gape-mouthed girl with embers. This made the women move, slowly at first, the one looking interestedly as the edges of her apron. Eyes wide with the implication, she emitted a small cry and began to pat at the smoldering cloth.

Her escort doubled back gathering Brenawyn and ushering her past the herd, "Back ta yer duties," she said to the room at large.

The corridor off the kitchen led directly to a steep staircase and Brenawyn was shepparded up. The utilitarian stair led up five flights and out on a walkway on the outside of the building where she looked over the entire picturesque compound and a river beyond. She wasn't allowed to enjoy it for long, though because the woman steered her to the corner turret. With the jingle of a key ring, she reached around Brenawyn, keeping a steel grip on her arm, to open the door.

Brenawyn stepped into the Spartan apartment. In it

was a large bed, stripped down to the bare linen rush mattress, a serviceable desk, and a bookshelf stuffed with tomes and scrolls in a higgly-piggly fashion.

The woman looked abashed at the state of the room, "Please forgive us, lady, I will find the lass responsible for this. Do ye like me ta bring her so ye can exact punishment?"

Brenawyn was confused. "Punishment?"

"Aye, I will order yer rooms ta be made presentable." She looked around the room with efficiency, mumbling to herself, checking off a mental list of supplies. She went to the empty fireplace, knelt, and in minutes a flame caught on the kindling. She fed it slowly, laying first a pile of thin branches, making sure they caught, and then laid the largest of the split logs across, careful not to smother it.

Brenawyn watched her for a long moment, her back still turned, as she crouched there, absently wiping her hands on her skirt. Brenawyn turned to unpin the broach and the cloak slipped through her fingers to the floor; she was unaccustomed to the weight of the dyed wool. She collected it from the floor, folded it in half, placed it on the end of the bed, and set the broach on top of it.

The woman turned. "Please, allow me ta help ye undress."

Brenawyn stepped back and laughed, "I can handle it, thank you."

"I will leave ye then ta make arrangements." The woman looked back at her and sighed, tears glistening in her eyes before closing the door behind her.

"Wait," Brenawyn called but the key slid into the

rusty lock with a click as it slid home effectively making Brenawyn prisoner. She unzipped her pack, unfolding her garments still damp from the cave. She dragged the two ladder-backed chairs in the room over to the fire and laid the wet clothing over it to dry. She sat on the hearth rug and took off her boots, placing her bare feet as close to the fire as she could stand, the purple polish on her toes a visual reminder that she didn't belong here. Why did she think that she should come? To what purpose? How was she to find Alexander in a time when any mention of Druid practice, or of Celtic gods would probably be misunderstood as witchcraft? Where was she to begin to look for Maggie?

Assess. What did she know? The two boys, the woman, and those who were in the kitchen knew of her presence. Add to that the guards in the tower—too many, considering by now more people had heard of the bundled stranger. She was locked in this room away from the other residents of the house, five floors up. It might as well be fifty stories up. The likelihood of escape seemed improbable. She'd just have to wait until a chance came her way.

The key rasped in the lock again and the door opened to a barrage of women carrying supplies—piles of linen and down comforters, tapestries, velvets, toiletries. A dozen women, most if not all had been in attendance in the kitchen, shyly dipped their heads and bowed, hurrying to ready the room. The woman who came in last in the line supervised as a brass tub that took four of girls to pull emerged from behind the partial wall. "Aye, and when done with that run ta get water heating on the brazier," she said.

The room was quickly swept, a feather bed fluffed and placed on top of the rush mattress and covered with linens and comforters. Velvet curtains were hung around the bed and tapestries over the windows to protect against drafts. Only then did the supervisor, Brenawyn's rescuer, turn to her with a smile on her face.

"I am Mistress Fordoun, I welcome ye ta the Keep."

"Nice to meet you, I'm Brenawyn McAllister."

She looked askance at Brenawyn but shook her head, "McAllister? Now, that t'is a surprise." Waving her hand, "No matter, t'is good ta be able ta put a name ta the sleeping lady."

"The sleeping lady? I think you have me confused … "

"Aye, the sleeping lady. Were ye not found in the glen sleeping by the fairy mound? Strange clothes. Aye, we've been waiting a long time for ye." She patted her arm, "Himself is out just the noo. Messengers ha' been dispatched. He will return, most like, 'afore a fortnight. Until then, yer every comfort will be seen ta, yer bath will be drawn and clothes set out for ye thaur," motioning to the bed. A pile of linen undergarments and several layers of what would constitute a dress in the current fashion, made of much richer fabrics than the ones on the women in the room lay over the back of the chair. Her own clothes were suspiciously absent. "Off with yer trews. Ye willna be needing them."

Brenawyn looked down, her trouble evidently written

on her flushed cheeks.

"Och, modest, are ye? Thaur is a screen yonder, undress thaur, and when the bath is ready I will call ye."

Much to Brenawyn delight, she saw that the screen was moveable and she repositioned it with little effort in front of the tub, went to the bed, carefully unfolded the undergarments and found what she hoped to be the first layer, was it called a shift in this time? She hung it over the top of the screen and then disappeared behind it.

The tub was deep and the water beckoned her with its steamy tendrils. She instructed the last of the girls, who wouldn't look her in the eye to leave the bucket. The girl, wild eyed, looked up shaking her head, casting looks over her shoulder at the main room that held the formidable Mistress Fordoun. "No, it's so I can rinse my hair."

"My lady, let me help ye, please," she whispered, still casting glances over her shoulder.

Brenawyn didn't know why, but she had the feeling that it would be worse for the girls if she dismissed all help. "All right." She knelt by the tub, unzipping the coveralls to her waist, her bra, the only thing she had underneath, another reminder that she was in a different time. The girl wouldn't know what to make of it. If she asked, it was a short corset designed to push up the breasts. Hopefully, she wouldn't look too closely at the details, eye hooks, and the maker tag. Jesus, Brenawyn was going to end up burnt at the stake.

The girl didn't say anything but reached for the pot of lavender scented soap and lathered it in, massaging her scalp and rinsed it with the bucket. Once done, Brenawyn stepped out of her garments and sunk into the tub, oblivious to everything but the still-steaming water. She sighed and closed her eyes.

When the water had finally cooled, she opened her eyes again. The girl was gone. A fluffy length of wool was folded on a chair by the tub, and Brenawyn got out and dried herself off. The noise brought the girl, wide eyed rushing around the screen, "My lady, ye should ha' called. T'is my job."

"Relax. I won't tell," she said, holding the towel around herself. "What is your name?"

"Me mum calls me Margaret," she answered in a high-pitched voice, hastily curtsying.

"Margaret," she said, dropping the towel, "was my mother's name. Can you help me dress?" This is what was customary, as awkward as it seemed. She needed to fit in, who knew who this girl would speak to after she left, besides she wouldn't be able to dress herself, after the shift.

~~~

An escort came to get her for dinner, a quiet affair with a smattering of people, most of whom she had seen on her arrival. This routine continued for ten days. She spent her days in the tower, at meals someone, usually one of the two boys who initially found her, would come for her, offer an arm, escort her down patiently waiting as she stumbled over her ill-fitting shoes, and be ready to take her again to her chambers afterward, but would not speak to her.

On the eleventh day, early, horns awoke her. She

pushed the tapestry aside and looked out the window, but it offered no view of what was happening below. She paced the apartment and when the door opened sometime later, it was to a flush-cheeked girl, eager to be away.

"What is happening? Who has come?"

"My da has come home. He was gone with the baron. They ha' come home early; they say ta see ye, my lady."

"Did you miss your father?"

The girl bounced up and down nodding her head, "My da brings me trinkets always."

"Then you should go to him."

"But … "

"No buts, sweetie, go find your father. I expect someone else will come for me."

She didn't have to wait long, Mistress Fordoun and her entourage came bustling in with toiletries and arms full of muslin and a gown. They whirled around pulling Brenawyn to her feet but that was all the effort she needed to make, all else was done for her. The shift was whisked off her head and new fine lawn one replaced it. A corset came around her and Brenawyn thought she'd pass out; she couldn't breathe or sit. "No' ta worry, my lady, yer going ta be beautiful."

By the time she was plunked down on a stool in front of the mirror, she didn't recognize herself. The corset whittled her waist to an impossible state, pushing her breasts up until they teetered on the edge of popping out any moment. She hoped not. The boning would probably do irreparable damage to her. The person who cut the strings on this thing would have her undying gratitude, if

MELISSA MACFIE

they burned it with all the rest of these horrid corsets, she'd have his baby. How many years had she complained about the underwire in her bras? It was nothing in comparison to this. The thought made her giggle. *Oof, no giggling either.*

Her hair was brushed by two women, clucking and arguing amongst themselves over the style. They opted to braid it into tiny sections, weaving the braided ropes, so they fit snug against the back of her head, the remainder left to cascade down her back. They left in a hurry leaving Brenawyn with Mistress Fordoun. She hung in the back, distractedly playing with the leaves of flowers set for the braided coiffure.

"The man of the house is home? What can I expect?"

She shook her head, "I doona ken, my lady. Depends on how the request is answered. I had the boys send a note ta their da asking for a private audience. They ha' ta present ye ta court, but ye couldna ha' come at a worse time, my lady. We are a house divided. T'is no' a tolerant time. The auld ways are dying and ye could be in danger. Thaur has been talk o' burnings."

"Then help me get out. I came to find the Merlin. I don't know how I'll locate him but my chances are better out there than in here behind lock and key waiting for God knows what. Help me."

She dragged a chair over to the door and shoved it under the handle and came back to kneel in front of Brenawyn. "My lady, doona fear the master o' the house. He is compassionate ta yer plight, but gifted he is no'. Doona mention the Merlin, gone these past twenty years, left o' a sudden with no word. A day hasna passed without the Sinclair weeping over the loss o' his brother. A sad fate for the entire clan, the witch hunters rose in this area decades ago and it was decided ta hide Alexander, once he showed the gift. They sent him off ta learn, but publically wiped his existence ta the rest o' the world. Deid in childhood it says on the tombstone o' an empty grave.

"It would ha' stayed that way, had Alexander no' come back. A strong braw lad he had grown inta, made me weep ta see him again, want ta keep him safe as I had done for all his life, but I couldna. He had grown beyond my help, the markings on his chest."

Brenawyn grabbed her arms, "What do, did, they look like?"

"An ancient script in deepest indigo," she leaned forward whispering, "Marking him a Druid, one of the Tuatha de Dananns' own."

Close, but no mention of the red, Brenawyn sat back disappointed, the name and the markings too much of a coincidence to ignore, but she berated herself for hoping that she had been brought to Alexander's family. That would be too easy.

"He didna keep a low profile; he couldn't naturally, looking so much like his brother, quite the formidable, the two o' them, and with his markings, which he made no move ta hide. Very close the two o' them were, inseparable, always ta be found practicing in the lists, his markings out for the world ta see.

Thaur are so many visitors to these parts, it was a growing concern, and it was only a matter of time before attention would be drawn ta the keep. Alex wouldna ha' gone willingly, his brother at his back in defense, making it worse for the family, but thank the gods he wasna haur when they eventually came. The examiners overstayed their welcome within a day but lingered and once they'd gone, the traitor was dealt with."

"So what happens if your request is denied?"

"It may be. I couldna trust ta put inta words what has happened, who ye are."

"Who you think I am."

She brushed this off inconsequentially, "I need ta think o' a way ta explain ye. The boys, gods love them, are boys. Who kens who ha' heard the story o' yer discovery? The odd way ye were dressed, yer speech. Aye, a convincing story will have ta be supplied, if ye are presented publically. Mind ye, ye'll end up that way, but the Sinclair needs ta ken about ye first ta decide what's ta dae with ye."

A knock at the door had Mistress Fordoun scurry to ease the chair away. Once she had replaced it in a location that didn't look suspiciously like it had been used as a safeguard against entry, did she open the door. A young man, just old enough to grow a first, scraggly beard, stood at the door. "Mistress Fordoun, yer presence is required downstairs. I am ordered ta bring yer guest presently."

His words hung in the air and a panic settled in the pit of Brenawyn's stomach. She would be going down alone. "

Mistress Fordoun turned to her before exiting, "Take heart, my lady, I will speak for ye."

It was a relief, but she had to make the descent with

this young man she had never seen before, his armament, the sword held in the scabbard at his back, and the blade tied to his thigh, a clear indication that she was in trouble. As she followed him down to the dining hall, all desire for small talk dried in her throat. No need to discern information when the prospect of finding too much about her tenuous situation in a few mere minutes seemed too much to bear. She assessed the various exits, archways giving to nothing more than another stone hallway, what was beyond, out of her sight. A flurry of activity was in progress, the floors were being swept and scrubbed, and trestle tables brought in, tallow candles replaced by fresh, the busy set up for a feast for the lord returned home.

Without turning to see if she followed, the man walked through a small opening at the back of the dais and took winding stairs. She slowed her steps, knowing she was walking further away from any escape. "Doona think about it, lass, I'd be on ye, 'afore ye made the nearest archway. Come, it won't be bad," said the man, his attention attracted by the change in her gait.

Brenawyn looked at him, trying to hide her thoughts; she was quick normally, out of this contraption called fashion. She couldn't get a deep breath, she was seeing spots in front of her eyes, by the slight exertion of the climb, and he was faster in all probability. Possessing the upper body strength to use that sword, his legs were knotted with muscle. No, she couldn't outrun him. She smiled sweetly into his face, using her looks to distract. From the resulting look on his face, the gambit worked. She followed him up the stairs to meet whatever fate the universe threw her into.

A knock at the oak door granted them entry, but her escort smiled at her, opening it for her but didn't enter himself. She heard the door click closed and softly bang against its frame as if he taken his place, back up against it, to guard.

"Would ye like some sherry, lass?"

Brenawyn turned to face the voice, "No, thank y ... oh God, Alex?" Taking two steps toward him. The hair greying at the temples marked him as only a close relative after the words were out of her mouth. Urgings from Fordoun screamed in her head. *Oh God. Oh God.* "I apologize. You look like someone I knew."

He got up from the chair and walked over to her, around her, she felt his eyes boring into her. He stopped in front and lifted her chin to look into her eyes. "Ken my brother, dae ye?"

"I, uh, um, I do, I think." She looked into eyes the same shade, focusing on the graying hair at the temples. This was not Alex.

"Taller than myself, wider in the shoulder, same eyes as our mother, and though yer no' likely ta ha' seen, but I have ta ask, dae ye know if he had um ... scars, um, on his ... chest?"

"Not scars but something else."

"Markings in blue, and red the newest addition, the last time I saw him?"

"Oh, God." she sobbed in relief, "You are his brother."

"Tell me, when did ye last see him? Whaur? Is he in

214

good health? Tell me."

She wanted to tell him everything, to release the burden of holding everything in, all the fantastic, and unbelievable; she wouldn't have believed if it didn't happen in front of her eyes. Caution held her back. What should she tell him? The last time she saw him, what could she reveal without giving hint to the otherworldly. She'd hold that for now, the whole experience and focus on the image of him standing amid their camp, shirtless promising more pleasure; she felt the blood rise to her cheeks, "He was well when last I saw him, not too long ago."

He chuckled, "Aye, t'is good ta hear that he still has that effect on the lasses." He hugged her to his chest, "Thank ye for giving me news on my brother, Alexander. Tell me, is he coming home soon."

He must have felt her stiffen, because he gave a small cry and hugged her harder, "Forget I asked. Doona tell me." Trembling he set her away from him. "Let us focus on the immediate. I doona kin what ye expect o' us, but some explanation needs ta be given for ye. Dae ye mind being named as Mistress Fordoun's niece? All know she has family a ways off."

"I mean to be gone soon."

"With no guard, nothing o' yer own?"

"I know that these are borrowed, but if I could have my clothes I arrived in back."

"Impossible. They were destroyed, burned ta prevent anyone learning o' the circumstances o' yer arrival."

"All of my clothes?"

"For yer own safety, aye. Doona fear, though, ye are in no danger from the likes o' this house. All will be well. Ye may stay in my solar until yer formal presentation ta me. I will be granting ye asylum. Under penalty o' death, would anyone dare ta touch ye." He grabbed her hand and kissed it. "Until later, my dear." He turned on his heel, the cape billowing out behind him. The door openly automatically by the same guard who brought her there, to allow the lord passage from his apartments.

CHAPTER 17

Brenawyn had to stand public presentation, whatever that entailed. Hopefully, it stood on formal ceremony, not much time for unanswerable questions. Let Fordoun claim her as niece, she'd have to remember to ask her given name before this ruse came to a screeching halt but if accepted by the populace here, it wouldn't seem amiss if she had more freedom and access to the outside world.

Time passed slowly but when the door opened, Brenawyn wished she had more time alone with her thoughts. The young guard again escorting her. The hall had undergone a transformation in her absence mostly due to the people crammed cheek to jowl in the expansive space. They didn't enter through the same archway, he took her along another pass, circuitously circumventing the crowd until at last they came into the room behind everyone else, then moving close to the elevated dais. She

217

was tall enough to see over most heads to where Lord Sinclair sat with his sons, the boys that she had first met, both of whom looked bored. Their father, reserved, sat in the ornate chair, waiting until the murmur died down. He stood and a hush swept the crowd, "T'is good to be home," to a raucous cheer resounding off the rafters.

"My lord," at first he wasn't heard, Brenawyn only did because the man was a few feet away from her. He cleared his throat, "My Lord!" louder. The people around him shushed but gave him a look. He stepped forward, pushing the crowd out of his way. She could hear grunts of resistance, and an occasional yelp, but the unknown man gradually made his way to the front to garner the attention of Sinclair. "Yes?"

"I beg pardon, my lord, but a most distressing piece of news made it to mine ears. Can ye confirm that the sleeping lady has been found by yer own sons?"

Silence reigned; the only movement was the craning of Sinclair's neck to look at his boys, who had identical looks of fear on their faces. "But da, we only … "

"Hush now. Off with ye. I'll find ye later." Waiting patiently for the boys to get up, he did not turn back to the questioner until they departed. By then, whispers of the sleeping lady made it back to Brenawyn. She wanted to run. The crowd packed closer together when he opened his mouth to speak, pulling her into the tide of its rush. There was nowhere to go. The guard was miraculously still next to her.

He took her by the arm; she could feel through the fabric of her dress that his knife was no longer in its sheath.

"Hush, let me hear." Too distracted by the knife clutched in his free hand, she didn't care who the lady was, her only thought was why he thought to pull his knife. There was danger here.

"Tell me true, my lord. Shall we rejoice that trying times are at an end? Do the portents tell of the end of the suffering and the wasting sickness with the coming of the sleeping lady? Tell us, my lord."

In the back of the room, her guard managed to wedge himself behind her, leaving her exposed. He leaned over. "Stay very still," he whispered, and slid the knife between her skin and the corset. "Can ye reach it?"

She nodded swallowing the tears that threatened. "Yes."

"Good. Always keep it with you."

"John." Sinclair found her in the crowd, but spoke to her guard, "John, bring our guest forward."

The crowd parted, most gawking at her. She's too young, that's no' her." Chanting, "The sleeping lady. The sleeping lady." One woman crushed her, pleading, pulling at her sleeve, "Please," depositing a child in her arms, "touch my child, say a prayer for her, heal her." The child wailed in her arms, could she help her? The child was rigid, back bent in pain, heart racing, pumping blood too fast. The head. The problem was in the baby's head. The crowd rushed them on, the woman trailed in her wake refusing to let go of her sleeve. Brenawyn had seconds before the child would be taken out of her hands. Her runes lit up and the crowd stepped back. She felt her guard leave her side, felt the dagger against the skin of her back, and heard the slide of metal on metal. Dagger and short sword at her back. If she could only … there it was, the damaged blood vessel, she felt it begin to heal. The child's headache ease. The little body relaxed against her. She looked around for the mother to find her prostrate on the ground beside her. She bent to give the child back to her, touching her arm as she squatted next to her. The woman looked up; face ashen, avoiding her eyes. Brenawyn forced the bundle back into her arms but the mother was resistant. "Listen, your child lives." Grabbing her chin and forcing her head down, the baby cooed, its fists waving happily in the air against her. The woman's eyes sprang open, "Ye ha' answered my prayers, milady. Oh thank ye, thank ye!"

The guard took Brenawyn's elbow and hauled her to her feet, "What ha' ye done, milady? What were ye thinkin'?"

"Silence." The word boomed out, Sinclair on the edge of the dais. "Bring her forward."

The last of the crowd parted and Brenawyn shook off the guard's steadying hand to walk alone to face the Sinclair publically.

"Milady." He bowed his head to her, and addressed the crowd, "t'is true, ye see before ye the sleeping lady. The one whose return the auld story foretold." Holding a hand to Brenawyn, "Come take yer place on the dais, milady."

Before she knew it, she was lifted onto the dais and physically turned to face the crowd, a strong hand on each shoulder, Sinclair, looking so much like Alex, put her in front of him.

"The priestess has come home."

People crowded the dais, cheek to jowl, trying to get a glimpse of her, their hands reaching for the hem of her skirts. She gripped the arms of her chair, her knuckles white. *Jesus, I can't control what people think, but to get them actual proof? What was I thinking? What have I done? I don't even know where I am.*

He must have felt her stiffen next to him, because he covered her ice cold hand with his warm one, enfolding it in his, and smiled at her. It was so like his brother's, they both smiled with their eyes, with one exception, there were deep laugh lines on her host's face.

Cheers went up from the room, but Brenawyn looked into the faces of those nearest the dais. Most were partaking in the general jovial ambiance, but there was a small handful that did not. Their faces were devoid of emotion, standing stock-still staring at her. One. Two. Three. Four. This was where the danger lay, with these four and however many more she did not see.

And I just marked myself as a Druid—a witch. They think me a witch! Shit.

Her host lifted her hand and placed a chaste kiss on her knuckles. He indicated with a flourish of his other hand, "Come, we must ha' music! T'is time for a celebration!"

The sure grip of the lord of the house gave her a shred of assurance, and she dared to look again into the sea of people. She met the eyes of a young woman. *Nope. Not confident enough to make eye contact with anyone else yet.* The room was large, and it was standing-room only. From her raised position she could see the four enormous fireplaces each with a fire blazing, located at equidistant points on the four walls. A new platform had been erected since her last visit to this room, on it the band stood readying themselves for another set. The instruments were different, but she recognized a few: the lute, bagpipes, one similar to a guitar but smaller, not as small as a ukulele— this was definitely the wrong part of the world for that, she thought.

They struck the first chord and off they went into the crowd in different directions, the music of their individual pieces to meet again blending in the rafters.

"We are lucky ta ha' Lughar and his troubadours settle in our lands. They ha' blessed us with their music and their tales, and 'til a time when my coin doesna lure them any longer, we'll enjoy the entertainment."

"He has a most pleasant voice, my lord."

"I am most pleased ta ha' ye say so."

The song ended with Lughar in front of the dais. He bowed to Sinclair and to Brenawyn in turn.

"Dae ye ken the devinalh[1] about the sleeping lady o' these parts, Lughar?"

"Aye, I dae. Shall I tell it then?"

"Please dae. The circumstances warrant a telling o' the auld story."

"One hundred years ago or more there was a battle; this battle was like none ye've e'er seen 'afore. T'was a battle within a battle. A battle for far more than land, more

---

[1] riddle

than wealth, more than position, more than honor!"

There was a communal snort of disbelief from the crowd.

"Aye, t'is true. On the surface, it may ha' seemed that way, but thaur was another, in the secret recesses … in the fairy mounds, a battle between forces no' o' this world."

The crowd melted from him, and his stage was laid bare. He was a storyteller true. He used movements, gesticulations, pauses, and the lone beat of a bodran somewhere off in the room. If anyone was a witch, it was him. He was mesmerizing. Children appeared at the edges of the circle made for him, sitting cross-legged at their parents' feet to hear his tale.

"On the surface men fought for the things that men always fight for. Bluid for bluid was shed; the earth was drenched in it. Laments echoed on the winds o' downed warriors: wives for husbands, mothers for sons, grandsons, children for fathers, grandfathers. So many laments the gods heard. The fighting fierce on land, the machinations cruel underneath, until they merged. Alliances made one to help the other defeat their foe, but they were made with short-sighted and daft men, those who couldna see the wolf. The rivers ran red with their bluid, ran red for three days; until the coming of Amergin."

Lughar paused for dramatic effect. He knew his crowd. They were entranced. Children excited, clutched their knees bouncing up and down, others pulled on the skirts and pants of the adults near. This was a favored story.

Amergin. Amergin? Can it be the same man from

Finvarra's stories? How common was that name?

"A wise one, was he, that Amergin. He played them, he did. Played the part o' the innocent lamb, like all those leaders o' men who had gone 'afore him. But he saw. He saw and he waited. He was part o' the first Accords meeting ta bring a truce, and still he waited for his moment."

"Tell us! Tell us!" a child shouted out.

"Aye, that I shall, my lad, that I shall." Lughar's voice took on a more melodic sound, and the stringed instruments sounded.

"A truce was signed, a false truce that day, ta wait nine waves distant from shore. Amergin saw the deceit in the eyes of those newly trusted. But still he remained mute. They did no' see his gift of Orpheus, so he ga' no' clues. Else they would no' ha' laid their plan. And when they set it in motion, the unearthly melody, his own voice rang out. Some say he had the voice to calm the beasts. Others say he had the strength to make the lasses swoon. I say … " The drum beat faster, "I say he had the power to command the elements!"

"He who calmed the storm! He who calmed the storm of the gods!" the children chirruped.

The rhythm slowed and quieted. "That he did. The waves eased, and then ceased to roll.

"The battle was fought on that shore and the second and a more lasting Accord was struck." Lughar stood in front of Brenawyn. "The omens foresaw it."

"The omens?" Brenawyn asked.

"When the last o' the kings o' the Tuatha Dé forfeit,

224

the night sky lit up as day in colors as vivid as the heather on the moor. The waters in the river ran clear again, the boar and the stag ran wild in the wood."

"Who was the interpreter of these omens?"

"Och, at first it was Caer Ibormeith, joined by her sister Aerten."

"But they are Tuatha Dé. How could their word be trusted?" There was a collective gasp from the crowd.

"Aye, my lady, ye are correct. They are Tuatha Dé, but then they are no'."

"Which is it? They cannot be both of them and not them."

Sinclair interrupted, "But they are both. Their combined word affects the gods and mortals alike. Prophecy and fate canna be denied. They are revered and hated both. There is nay way they can be corrupted: one without a mouth ta say nothing beyond what was prophesied, the other without eyes ta see anything beyond the prescribed fate."

"So what did they say of the omens?"

Lughar answered, "That a truce forged that day would hold until balance is lost. A new one only ta be restruck when the sleeping lady appeared again; and that only if she find what she seeks."

"So my lady, what is it that ye seek? And how may we help ye in yer quest?"

At that moment there was movement, and the crowd amiably parted. A tall, fair-haired man walked in, his head down. The over-sized linen shirt and baggy pants couldn't hide his lean muscular physique. Recognition dawned as she registered him as the father of the little girl who had come to Brenawyn's room; she clung now to his knees. She smiled. The girl must be happy that her father is home. The smile faded because something was off. The way he stood, his stance was peculiar. Feet planted a shoulders width apart, back poker straight, hands balled into fists. It reminded her of someone … he lifted his face to her.

The metallic taste of blood, a loose molar, I breathed in through my mouth—broken molar, an exposed nerve, but no pain there. The pain radiated lower, my back screamed, pressure on my stomach. That was me. I inhaled sharply to move, praying that I could still do it, dreading the wave of new explosions of agony once I did. A scream that hardly sounded like it came from within me escaped my lips. Sweating. Shaking. Assessing. Broken tooth and wrist. Hurt to breathe. Broken ribs? The baby! My hands went to my belly, hard as usual. Interminable seconds and … nothing. I pushed on my stomach expecting, praying for an answering pressure. None. I felt lower, my hand came back covered in blood.

The stairs creaked with his slow step. His face came into my field of vision. His strong brow and cheekbones, his dimpled chin, blue eyes I'd thought to be the color of the clear ocean, now the color of ice, devoid of all emotion.

Her mouth went dry, new beads of sweat formed on her brow, her heart felt like it would burst from her chest. "Liam!" Brenawyn hissed wrenching herself out from beneath Sinclair's grasp and pivoted away. "You're dead. I buried you, you son of a bitch!"

Liam vaulted onto the dais but was blocked by a

befuddled Sinclair. "Let me past! Ye may think ye found the priestess … they may think they've found the sleeping lady; but in truth t'is only my wife ye've found."

GLOSSARY

Celtic Gods, Goddesses, Creatures, & Places

Addanc: Welsh primordial giant

Aine: *(AHN yuh)* Irish goddess for fertility

Aerten: *(EYER ten)* Cornish, Welsh goddess of fate

Agrona: Celtic goddess of strife and slaughter

Amergin: (AYV-r-ghin) Milesian bard and Druid who sang a magical song that allowed his people to land safely in Ireland

Badb: *(Bahv)* Irish goddess of war, often assumes the form of the raven

Belanus: Celtic god of light

Blodevweld: *(blo-DOY-weth)* Betrayed her husband by supernatural means which led to his death.

Bres: *(BRESH)* Tyrannical ruler of the Tuatha Dé, defeated at the second battle of Magh Tuireadh

Caer Ibormeith: *(Keer YEW mayth)* Pan-Celtic goddess of dreams and prophecy

Conmaicne Rein: The site the Tuatha Dé Danann landed in Ireland.

Cernunnos: *(KER noo nohs)* Pan-Celtic god of the Hunt

Danu: Mother of the Tuatha Dé Danann; Mother Earth

Dearg due: (*DAH-ruhg DU-ah*)Irish female faerie known for seducing human men

Dian Cecht: *(DIE-an KET)* god of healing and regeneration

Finvarra: *(VEEN varra)* Irish High King of the gods

Fir Bolg: *(FEAR-bolg)* Settlers to Ireland who lived peacefully until the coming of the Tuatha Dé Danann and the first battle of Magh Tuireadh.

Formor: Magical race who settled in Northern Ireland. Fought against the Tuatha Dé Danann in the second battle of Magh Tuireadh.

Gancanagh:*(Gan-Kana)* Irish male faerie known for seducing human women, said to emit an addictive toxin

Mandred: Cornish god, draws the All Power to the one who speaks his name

Milesians: The last group of settlers to come to Ireland. After the third battle of Magh Tuireadh, a truce is made where they would occupy the upper world, whereas the Tuatha Dé, the world below.

Neit: *(NYIT)* Irish god of battle

Nimue: *(NIM oo ay)* Cornish, Welsh goddess of the moon

Nuada: *(NEW-ah)*Twice king of the Tuatha De' Danann

Oghma: (OH-wam), Scottish/Irish god of communication and writing; known for inventing writing. In the Celtic Prophecy series, the god of memory.

Ratis: Anglo-Celtic goddess of protective fortifications

Sidhe: *(She)* Irish descendants of the Tuatha Dé Danann

Sluagh: restless spirits of the dead; in Fate's Hand, embodied as hounds

Sreng: *(share-EN)*Fir Bolg warrior who cut off Nuada's arm in the first battle of Magh Tuireadh

Taliesin: *(tal-YES-in)* Welsh god of magic, music, poetry, wisdom, and writing

Taranis: *(TA ran is)* Continental goddess of death to

whom sacrifices were offered.

Tir-Na-Nog: *(TIER na noog)* realm of the gods

Tuatha Dé Danann: *(TOO-ha dey DAHN-en)* Children of the goddess Danu

Gaelic Words and Phrases

a chuisle: *(a khish la)* term of endearment meaning my heart.

Eiliminteach: *(EE le men tie k) Elemental*

Fire Feasts

Samhain: *(SAH wen)* Celebrated on October 31 marking the beginning of winter

Oimelc: *(I melg)* Celebrated on February 1 marking the beginning of spring

Beltaine: *(BEY al TIN ah)* Celebrated on May 1 marking the beginning of summer

Lughnasadh: *(LOO nah sah)* Celebrated on August 1 marking the beginning of autumn

References

Celtic Gods and Goddesses
    http://www.joellessacredgrove.com/Celtic/deities.htm
    l
    22 June 2016.

Celtic Shamanism.
http://www. sacredfire.net/shaman.html 5 July 2016.

The Howe Caverns.
http://www.howecaverns.com/index.php.
22 June 2016.

"Howe Caverns Unveils New Discovery Tour Opening Areas of Cave Not Seen in 100 Years."
http://howecaverns.com/files//Howe-Media-Day-OnSite-Materials-4-21-15.pdf. 22 June 2016.

"Races." *Magic and Mythology.*
http://www.shee-eire.com/Magic&Mythology/Races/Page1.htm
13 June 2016.

Samuels, Jerry. "They're Coming to Take to Me Away."
1966.   http://www.songfacts.com/detail.php?id=675.
22 June 2016.

Spence, Lewis. *Druids: Their Origins and History.* United States of America. Barnes & Noble Books. 1995.

Squire, Charles. *Celtic Myths and Legends.* Bristol. Parragon. 1998.

Wood, Juliette. *The Celtic Book of the Living and Dying: The Illustrated Guide to Celtic Wisdom.* New York. Chartwell Books, Inc. 2012.

Look for

ORACLE'S CURSE
BOOK THREE OF
THE CELTIC PROPHECY

COMING IN 2017

A Message From the Author

   This past year has been exciting as I began, in earnest, to explore the world of publishing and marketing my fantasy series, The Celtic Prophecy. With the release of Fate's Hand and Reliquary's Choice ten months apart, I've learned the most rewarding aspect of this venture has been building a relationship with my readers. In the months to come I will be sending out newsletters alerting readers to sales, contests, and new releases. By going to my website, https://melissamacfie.com and subscribing to my newsletter you will receive an advance short of the next novel in The Celtic Prophecy series, *Oracle's Curse*. The short preview should be ready for release in December, 2016. You can also connect with me at www.facebook.com/celticprophecy where I periodically publish excerpts, list my appearances, and giveaways.

   A review is the most valuable gift you can give an author. Honest reviews are an invaluable tool for authors, helping them to become recognized for their work and helping them to connect with readers who are looking for new authors and interesting new books to read. If you enjoyed this book, I would whole-heartedly appreciate it if you'd take the time to leave a review when you reach the review link at the end of this book. If you do write one, please send me an email at melissa.macfie@yahoo.com so I can thank you personally.

Melissa Macfie

Acknowledgements

Artistic license was used in choosing the gods featured in this novel. While they are all of Celtic origin, they are not from the same country of origin. This was intentional to further diversify names. A list of gods and their specific origins are in the glossary.

I would like to acknowledge the anonymous aid I received from the Irish Translation Form on the Irish Gaelic Translator website. Their translations lend a nuanced authenticity to this novel. The responsibility for any incorrect usage or phrasing falls to me.

I would also like to acknowledge the tremendous encouragement and support I received from my friends, especially Maria Vazquez Gesumaria, Trish Buckley, Dr. Andrea Bassie, Diane Lang, John Nartowitz, Dr. Jack Bradley, Ruth Dershowitz, Ana Cunha, Sebastiano Stellato, and Manuela Sampedro. Thank you for requesting progress updates, listening to me, more times than not, doubt whether I could get the book finished by deadline, and who thankfully reminded me that I needed to enjoy life and not take myself too seriously. A special, heart-felt thank you goes out to the Thirsty Thursday crowd; our weekly meetings kept me sane.

Lastly, I would like to acknowledge my family, starting with my husband, Donald Andrew Macfie Jr., to whom this book is dedicated. If ever there was a man supportive of his wife, then he is it. He is patient and generous, picking up additional responsibilities with nary a complaint. I realize that I am a chore to live with especially, though more often if I'm being truthful, when I am finishing a book. I grow more inward, distant, and filled with self-doubt; but he was always there championing my efforts, bolstering my self-esteem, and making me laugh.

My daughter, Elizabeth, continues to be a sounding board for character development and story progression. Without her, I'd be stuck in the first fifty pages of Fate's Hand, knowing where I wanted to go but seeing no path to get there. If any of my readers have an issue with the characters—blame her. I jest! I can see her reaction as she eventually reads this. Seriously though, she helps me wade through the miasma, and see how and why things happen as they do.

My son, Donald, encourages me to strive for greater heights, periodically checking in to review whether I am following through on the marketing plan for my series laid out by my publisher, Karen Hodges Miller. He is a marketing major, so it's not as strange as it sounds. Those calls usually happen after midnight, which probably is the most productive time in the day for both of us when the minutia of the day ceases and we are left with just our thoughts. He is probably thankful I didn't have any questions on the male point of view for this book, though I can safely say that it was just a temporary reprieve.

No matter what else I achieve in this life, being a mother is my greatest accomplishment.

About the Author

For most of her life, Melissa Macfie has pursued artistic endeavors such as drawing, painting, and sculpting. She holds a M.Ed. in English Education from the Graduate School of Education at Rutgers University, and has spent the last sixteen years as a public school English teacher. She lives in New Jersey with her husband, Donald. Their children, Elizabeth and Donald, are grown and pursuing their own dreams.